Goldie,

These also are special words.

God Bless,

Dennis

And in the End, Love

Dennis E. Coates

WestBow Press books may be ordered through booksellers or by contacting:

WestBow Press
A Division of Thomas Nelson
1663 Liberty Drive
Bloomington, IN 47403
www.westbowpress.com
1-(866) 928-1240

ISBN: 978-1-4497-8479-9 (sc)

Library of Congress Control Number: 2013902577

Printed in the United States of America

WestBow Press rev. date: 02/12/2013

To

my grandchildren

Note:

The stories herein are fictional and intended for illustration.

Contents

Chapter 1

WHAT END?

One meaning of "the end" is what happens upon death. In this meaning, we consider what happens immediately after death. What happens to us? What happens to the soul? What happens to the body? What is the afterlife like? Will we know those we have loved in life? Will we be able to pray for those still on earth? What will God be like? Will I see Jesus face-to-face?

Or what will purgatory be like? How long will we be in purgatory? And what if heaven or purgatory is not my outcome? What will hell be like?

Another end is the end of the day or the end of a phase or project. It has to do with this life. But more specifically, it has to do with what it all means. Why do I do the things I do? If I live now without heaven, what does it mean? Can

I live now in heaven and on earth? How do the two relate to one another? Where do the two intersect? Is this of any real consequence to me?

Is there such a thing as heaven without hell? Does the existence of one imply—even necessitate—the other? Does the definition of one define the other? Do we have evidence in this life for the existence of each?

The end spoken of here is the end in the sense of purpose and consequence. Whether in the now or in the future, what is the end toward which our lives are going, whether by the end of the hour, the day, the year, or the life? What is the fruit of our lives? What is the effect of our lives? What is the outcome of the purpose we have given to our lives? What end are we moving toward?

In this sense of *end*, each of our ends is somewhat predetermined by who we are now. If I am devoted to my family, the fruit will have something to do with my family and not something else. If I am devoted to business, the fruit will be in the business. What I am devoted to will predetermine where the fruit of my effort will come to pass. This is somewhat self-evident. For example, if I devote no time to helping people in a foreign country, I will bear no fruit in that country. On the other hand, if I devote myself to helping people in my local community, that is where the fruit of my effort will become reality.

There is, however, a larger sense of the fruit of my life that is unconnected to my effort or where I devote my time. That is in the area of character. My character affects everyone around me, no matter where I am devoting my effort and time. It affects my family, my friends, and my colleagues. Character is like a dye that changes the color of water when introduced into it. Who I am affects others in my life and in ways that are largely outside my notice.

Here we come closer to the nature of the term *end* as intended here. What is the end in sight for who I am? Who will I be at the end of the day, the year, and my life? In this sense, the end is always a future event. I am something now, and I am becoming something. What will that something be? In the end, who do I want to be? What do I want to be? Why do I want to be that?

When I was a boy, I wanted to be a bus driver. When I was a teen, I wanted to be a teacher. I thought of myself in terms of the work I might do in life. I didn't think of myself in terms of character—who I wanted to be as a person. Nor did I ever think of why I would want to be this or that in terms of character. I was just who I was, and that was that. No thought was given to it. In the end, who I was or would become was up to chance, events, or something else—but not up to me. I wouldn't have known what my choices were. I wouldn't have known how to direct my becoming.

What were the choices? If I were to consciously decide what I would become in terms of the formation of my character as a person, what was the language surrounding that issue? What words were available to begin to think about it? If we don't have a framework of thought, how can we even begin to understand the choices available?

Let's begin somewhere. Suppose I want to be a "nice" person who is liked by all. That could be a goal I set for myself. And what could be wrong with that? Wouldn't everyone want to be liked by all? That goal would set the framework for how I would seek to live; it would establish the guideline I would follow to become the kind of person

I wanted to become. I would try to determine what kinds of things I could do that others would like or admire. Perhaps I would read books on how to become popular, on how to win friends and influence people. Perhaps I would learn how to throw good parties everyone wanted to come to.

But what if I were a person who wanted to be taken seriously? Perhaps this would help me to become a successful person who would be respected as an up-and-comer in business or in my profession. I would be seen as diligent, intense, and committed. This is how I would lead my life. I would be seen as I really am—a committed, serious person who will be just what some people are looking for. I wouldn't be seen as a nice person but one who could actually get things done.

On the other hand, once I begin to get the idea of how this is done from examples like the ones above, I could decide that I don't want to be a nice person or a serious person. Instead, I want to be a giving person. A giving person is one who is always aware of the needs of others and seeks to meet those needs. That is what I choose to become. I will always try to determine the needs of others, and I will try to meet those needs. That sounds like a really good kind of person to become, so that is what I will try to become as a person. I will form that habit so deeply that it will become second nature to me. When that happens, that is who I will actually be.

Do you think this is true to life? Is this actually the process by which we become the persons we are or will become? It's partly true but not true in the core of its meaning.

The truth is closer to this. We are already persons in our inner being, and the experience of life keeps bringing us closer in touch with who we are. It's more a process of discovery of who we are as persons. We have natural interests and capacities that mark who we are. With each experience of life, our personalities come out and develop. Each of us discovers how unique an individual he or she is, with certain gifts and capacities. We discover that when we do things in life that bring out and develop these aspects, we come closer to discovering that happiness is a consequence.

I could decide I want to be a serious person, but if I am not serious by nature, no amount of my effort to become so will do me much good because, simply, it's not who I am. I cannot arbitrarily change who I am without doing damage to myself as a person.

This has to do with developing natural interests and capacities. What about the area of natural capacity that involves faith, hope, and love? This is an area of life that is common to every human being, and these have much to do with who we are and who we become as persons. The opposite is true as well. We all have a natural capacity for unbelief, hopelessness, and lovelessness. These too have much to do with who we are and who we become as persons.

Values also have much to do with who we are and who we become. A person who sees other people as valuable will treat them accordingly; those who do not will treat them accordingly. Persons who hold the family as valuable will treat them so. Persons who hold truth as valuable will not lie; those who do not will find it easier to lie.

All these things go into the making of the persons we become. In the end, we will be the persons we have been predetermined to be by the combination of these things that are active in our lives. Some are at work because of who we already are as persons by DNA, and some will be the consequence of decisions we make, or fail to make, about our own lives. In the end, we will be what we are becoming. Here's a story that illustrates this.

Ed was a young man in his early twenties. He was almost finished with university, and all had gone fairly well. Ed was a casual, likable guy who had a good idea of where he wanted to go in life. He knew he had mathematical skills, and he loved to think precisely about things. Engineering suited him perfectly, and this was confirmed in his grades. He had also been accepted into a large engineering firm when he graduated, so he knew exactly where he was going in the immediate future.

Ed came from a family that had no religious beliefs, and thus he never had any upbringing related to the church. His understanding of religious things was minimal and limited to what he had learned in school in courses of comparative religion. He knew no one among his circle of friends who had deep religious faith and therefore had no real religious influence in his life. Thus it was that religious considerations found no place in Ed's thinking about the kind of person he wanted to be.

Ed had never experienced any serious problems in life, medically, socially, or academically. His was a contented life marked by freedom from trauma or grief. None of his family members had died, so he had never been confronted by the death of a loved one. He had never had to experience failure or radical change in his life due to loss of income or job.

Ed had a girlfriend he had met in school. It couldn't be described as a deep love affair; neither of them saw marriage as part of their relationship or future. But they enjoyed each other's company, and this level of relationship was just fine for each of them.

In terms of the development of Ed's character, the ingredients at play were: a loving and comfortable home and upbringing; a recognition of skills that he put to use in his education; a future that appeared secure in work that he liked; and a disposition that could be described as content and that had not yet experienced grief or trauma in life. His ideas of what a person should be were that one should be a good person, likeable, well adjusted, and using his talents as best possible. He wanted to be diligent in his endeavors and progress in his chosen career. He hadn't given much thought at this point to marriage or family, nor to how he wished to raise his children. Absent too from his thought was any real consideration of meaning in life or why he existed at all. Life, for Ed, just happened.

Let's now fast forward ten years in Ed's life and get a glimpse of what his life has become and where he is going as a person.

Ed was married now and had two young children. He had met his wife, Shelley, at a friend's party one night, and the two hit it off immediately. They began to date, and within two years, they had married. It was a civil marriage attended by a few friends and family members. Each of them had a career that was progressing very well. Ed was now a senior engineer in the same firm, and Shelley was a dietician at the local hospital. She, too, had had no religious upbringing and like Ed, had never had a need to question the purpose of life or its meaning. Like Ed, life for her had always just happened. The two of them continued to approach life in this vein each day.

Ed was content, happy with his wife, and happy with their children, Amy and Ryan. If asked how he was doing, he would answer, "Very well indeed; life doesn't get better than this." His disposition was a constant, his goals in life the same. He was a good person, likeable, well adjusted, diligent, and using his talents as best possible, and so was Shelley. From his point of view, there was no need for God, for deeper questioning about life, or for concern for the future.

This all changed within the space of one year. Both of Ed's parents died that year, and Shelley's father died as well. Amy had a life-threatening illness that hospitalized her in intensive care for over a month. Ed, for the first time in his life, experienced grief at the loss of his parents. For the first time in his life, he experienced the trauma of the near death of a child. And in addition to this, neither Ed nor Shelley was completely able to help the other with their grief or worry.

One night Ed said to Shelley, "What if Amy had died? Would her life have meant anything? What about my parents? They just lived and died. They didn't believe in anything beyond the day. Each of them died without ever attaching any significance to their existence. Did their lives mean anything? I don't know what to make of all that has happened in the past year. I realize that in all my life, I've never really thought about these things. Surely, Shelley, there must be some meaning to people's lives. Surely we can't just live and die and that's it. I think of Amy, and the thought that her life would have no significance just doesn't make any sense to me. This has really been troubling me lately, and I have to try to find some answers."

Shelley replied, "I have to say, it's troubled me too. But I wasn't thinking in terms of the significance of Amy's life or that of our parents. I was thinking of it in terms of my love for her. If she had died, there would have been a huge hole in my heart, and I don't know what I would have done. I asked myself how people ever get over the death of a child. I just can't imagine it. I would have been angry about it and frustrated that I couldn't do anything. I would have been angry at the injustice of it. Why should a little girl die? It doesn't seem right to me. And if there were a God, why would God allow these kinds of things to happen? Those are the kinds of thoughts and feelings I've had. It makes me mad that we almost lost her."

Afterward, Ed thought about their conversation. *Is that all I'd do—feel angry? What would that solve? It wouldn't bring her back. It wouldn't answer my questions. It would just leave me angry, without a way of dealing with the issue itself. I wouldn't know what significance Amy's life had or that of each of my parents. That's no good. I can't simply leave it that way. I need some answers.*

Chapter 2

WHY LOVE?

If I have all the eloquence of men or of angels, but speak without love, I am simply a gong booming or a cymbal clashing. If I have gifts of prophecy, understanding all the mysteries there are, and knowing everything, and if I have faith in all its fullness, to move mountains, but without love, then I am nothing at all. If I give away all that I possess, piece by piece, and if I even let them take my body to burn it, but am without love, it will do me no good whatever. Love is always patient and kind; it is never jealous; love is never boastful or conceited; it is never rude or selfish; it does not take offence, and is not resentful. Love

> takes no pleasure in other people's sins but delights in the truth; it is always ready to excuse, to trust, to hope, and to endure whatever comes. Love does not come to an end. But if there are gifts of prophecy, the time will come when they must fail; or the gift of languages, it will not continue forever; and knowledge - for this, too, the time will come when it must fail. For our knowledge is imperfect and our prophesying is imperfect; but once perfection comes, all imperfect things will disappear. When I was a child, I used to talk like a child, and think like a child, and argue like a child, but now I am a man, all childish ways are put behind me. Now we are seeing a dim reflection in a mirror; but then we shall be seeing face to face. The knowledge that I have now is imperfect; but then I shall know as fully as I am known. In short, there are three things that last: faith, hope and love; and the greatest of these is love.[1]

Why love? Because love is the very essence of God. If God is not love, then the action of Christ cannot be understood, and if Christ is not understood, we cannot understand why he came or what motivated him. Without love, we cannot understand our own selves properly, for we are able to love, and without love, we shrivel and die. Without understanding that love is at the heart of all true understanding, we cannot understand why we are able

1 1 Corinthians 13:1–13. Note: Scriptural references are from *The Jerusalem Bible*, Reader's Edition. (Garden City, New York: Doubleday & Company, Inc., 1968).

to love or that we are called to love or that we are made in the image of God. God is love, and we are made in his image. The nature of God—who is love—is revealed in Jesus Christ, true God and true man.

The questions Ed asked in the previous chapter will be difficult to answer in the absence of a background of some sort in Christianity. His is the type of question that begins the search for answers that are true, that fulfill, and that do not mislead. All the questions we have ultimately seek truth.

How can Ed find the truth? Where can he find it? To whom can he go? How difficult will his quest be? Will he stick to it long enough to find the truth that sets free, that shows what life is about, that offers the proper basis for faith, hope, and love that will not let us down or lead us astray?

Let us follow Ed's story.

Ed had a high school friend who went on to become a priest. He was the only person Ed could think of who might begin to answer his questions. Through some inquiries, Ed discovered his friend, now Fr. Jim, was the pastor of a parish in a nearby city. Ed called him and made an appointment.

When he met with Fr. Jim, Ed told him that his number-one question was about the meaning of life. He told Fr. Jim about his parents and his daughter's near-death experience and that these were the events that, for the first time in his life, had gotten him thinking about the meaning of life.

"Surely, Jim, my daughter's life means more than just a 'coming and going, enjoy it while you can' kind of thing.

And if there is meaning, what is it in terms of making my daughter's life worthwhile and significant? And for that matter, my own and my wife's? Where do I begin? And when I begin, how can I get the right answers? How will I know I'm not spinning my wheels, wasting my time? Do you think you can help me?

"I've never had any religious upbringing whatsoever, so I don't know what Christianity actually is about apart from a general knowledge that Jesus Christ is at the heart of it. I'm more of the school of thought that accepts that every religion has its point of view and that each contains its element of truth. But if I am to seek answers through religion, which one offers *the* truth I can stake my life on? Which one can assure me that it has the answers I'm looking for?"

"Wow," answered Fr. Jim, "those are some pretty important questions and considerations. How do I begin to answer you and to assure you that Christ is the answer to *all* your questions, no matter what they are? Let me begin with some assurance along those lines—that Christ is the answer and that you need look no further than him. Indeed, if you look elsewhere for the answer, you will have missed the bull's-eye.

"Let me begin with a question: how would one determine truth? What criteria would one use to assess if something is the truth? How would one know if something claiming to be the truth is actually a deceit?

"Here are some thoughts on that. The first would be: Does the claim stand the test of time? Also, does the test include millions of people over hundreds of years? Is the claim related to the reality of human experience?

Is the claim something that can be subjected to the test of human reason? Does the claim have any authority behind it?

"I think these few questions will help you in sifting truth from falsehood. Let's take a simple example of a claim that didn't stand the test of time: the belief that the earth is the center of the universe. Science showed conclusively that this is not true—that the earth itself is in orbit around the sun and that this solar system is just a small part of one galaxy, and this galaxy is just one among thousands.

"On the other hand, taken from a religious or philosophical point of view regarding the perceived importance of the human being to God, understanding what it means to be made in the image of God, one could say indeed that man, not the earth, is the center of the universe if he were the only such being created by God.

"So the test of time is important as one way of determining truth. In this regard, Christianity has been proclaimed openly throughout the world to millions of people over centuries. From the viewpoint of the test of time and numbers of Christians involved over a long period of time, many of whom suffered persecution and even death for the sake of their faith, Christian belief has stood the test. If anything, it has only grown more purified in its self-understanding through this time and experience.

"But even if you were to test Christianity throughout the world today, I think you would find that nothing has been so examined and expressed and taught and discussed as much as Christianity, by friend and foe alike. And still, its fundamental beliefs and understandings have not been shaken, its depth still not totally probed, its explanation of life not overthrown.

"From a personal point of view, for those who truly enter into its life, the fullness of Christianity is unmatched, in my view, as to enable the fulfillment of the deepest yearnings of the soul. I say this from my own experience and from my firsthand knowledge of many I know who would say the same thing.

"From all these things, I dare to say to you and to all who would hear me that Christ is the real thing. He is the Savior and Lord he is proclaimed to be, and you would not waste your time seeking him out where he is to be found. And where is that? In his church—the very church he created so he could dwell therein until the end of time and make himself available to all.

"That would be my answer to your question," Fr. Jim finished.

"Thanks, Jim. I trust you in your answer, and it makes sense to me. So where do I begin? How do I proceed?" Ed asked.

"I suggest you enter the RCIA, the Rite of Christian Initiation of Adults. It is precisely for people like you who have never been baptized. I suggest you go to the Catholic church nearest you and talk to the pastor about possibly entering the RCIA. The RCIA beings with an inquiry period so you can see how far you wish to go in the process. That would be my advice. And I suggest you talk to Shelley about this because she too may want to join you in this journey toward faith."

"I don't know about that," Ed responded. "She's pretty upset about the near death of our daughter. She doesn't seem very disposed to this kind of thing. It's me who is looking for answers, not her."

"Nonetheless," Fr. Jim said, "it would be good if the two of you could look into this together. It would provide a rock for the two of you in the way you live your lives and in the way you raise your family. At least talk to her about it. The RCIA involves a fair commitment of time and effort, but I'm sure you will find it answers your questions and gives you what you're looking for."

That night Ed told Shelley of his meeting with Fr. Jim and what he had suggested for the two of them.

"Why would I want to look into becoming a Catholic?" Shelley answered. "I'm not even interested in looking into religion. If you weren't looking into this, these thoughts would not even occur to me. So why would I want to do this? It's not making any sense to me."

"I know it's me who wants to know what the meaning of our lives is. I need to find this out, and I have to find a way to find it out. Fr. Jim's thought was that this could be a good thing for the two of us if we did this together. That's really what I'm hoping for, that you might join me in this for the sake of the two of us and for our family. If, after a while, you find that it's not for you, then at least you will have tried for my sake, and that's all I could ask of you."

"But why Catholic? Or even Christian? Why not simply a philosophical approach that might be able to satisfy you or maybe a course to take or a few books to read? Then when you get what you're looking for, you could share that with me and life could carry on."

"I guess I've come to the point where I want the truth about life and not just anyone's theory about it. I need something that is true and will not mislead me, something I can count on. That's what I'm looking for. Why Catholic? I never started out looking into Christianity or Catholicism. I just happened to know Jim and that he had become a priest. I went to him looking for some direction. I don't know if the RCIA is what I'm looking for at this point, but at least I know it exists and could be a starting point. I will take up his suggestion and go and see the local pastor. Maybe he can give me some further advice."

"Well," replied Shelley, "see what he has to say, and we'll talk about it then."

Ed called and made an appointment with Fr. Ben, the local pastor. When they met, Ed brought Fr. Ben up to date on what he was trying to do. He also told Fr. Ben what Shelley had said and that he now thought it was probably premature for them to consider the RCIA. He thought Shelley was likely right that some step had to come before that would be a consideration.

"I agree," said Fr. Ben. "Usually one enters the RCIA only when one feels drawn to look into entering the Catholic church, and from what you've said, this isn't really what you're looking for. I agree you could learn a great deal in the RCIA, but I think there's a better way for you at this point in time. You have to come to some basic understanding about God and life at this point in order to have a framework within which to think about things. That's what I would suggest to you as a starting point. This would also make it easier for your wife to understand what you're doing, and hopefully this might engage her thought process as well."

"So where would I begin, Father?" asked Ed.

"I have a book here I'd like you to read. It's called, *Why Love?*[2] I think this one book will give you a framework within which to consider all the things you've been asking. As you read it, try to be aware of the questions it may raise in you. Don't just let them slip by, because this is the kind of book this is. It will prod you into asking some very basic questions about life, love, and God."

Ed took the book home with him and began to read it that night.

---

2 Not an actual book

Chapter 3

HOW CAN I LOVE?

Ed found himself deeply engrossed in the book, and just like Fr. Ben had said, questions began to occur to him that hadn't before. He began to write the questions down so he could ponder them and try to find an answer. One question stood out among the rest, and he went to Shelley to ask her what she thought about it in the hope the two of them could try to find an answer.

The question was, "Why do we love?"

Shelley found the question interesting and was willing to join Ed in finding an answer.

"Why do we love?" Ed began. "I suppose I can't imagine life without love. We wouldn't be together if we didn't love. We wouldn't have been so concerned about Amy if we didn't feel love for her and didn't have the intelligence to know what her illness could mean to her and to us."

Shelley added, "And what about our parents? We know they loved us and that we loved them. Any parents we know love their children and their friends and their friends' children. Life without love doesn't make any sense. What would anything mean if we couldn't love?"

Ed responded, "But that shows that we need love; we need to love and to be loved. But the question is, 'Why do we love?' The simplest thing is that it's part of our nature as human beings; it's one of the things that identify us in terms of our nature, a major character trait of the human being."

"But isn't the question asking why we are like this?" responded Shelley.

"I think so," said Ed. "I don't know if I can go much further than we have. Why are we made this way? Was it just an accident, a freak of nature? If God made us, did he make us this way intentionally? If God didn't make us, how did we come to be so different than any other kind of being we know of?"

"Did you write down another question?" asked Shelley.

"Yes. The next one I had was, 'Why are men and women so different?' This came from part of the first chapter of the book that looked at the difference in the way men and women love. It showed the different kinds of needs men and women have and how each expresses these differences in the way they love and respond to love. This got me thinking about men and women more broadly, and that led to my question about why men and women are so different."

Shelley commented, "Are you sure you want to keep reading this book? Doesn't it provide the answers to any of these questions? I'm not sure I'd continue reading a book that only generates questions and doesn't provide any answers."

"Well, I think it will eventually provide some answers. It is called *Why Love?* I expect it to answer that question. In the meantime, Fr. Ben said I'd get more out of it if I note the questions it prompts. So why do you think men and women are so different? The first thing that comes to my mind is that women bear children and men don't. It seems to me women have to have some built-in ability to love their babies in ways men don't. That could be one reason."

"I think that's true," replied Shelley. "Women are the essential caregivers in a family, and we do have some innate abilities related to having children and raising them. But it seems to me that men have some characteristics that distinguish them from women. The first that comes to my mind is that men are attracted to women in different ways than women are attracted to men. They seem much more sexually driven than women are. I don't know if that's true or not, but it seems to me they are. That being the case, then the hormone difference between men and women must be what accounts for that."

Ed replied, "In any event, it's good they are different. Look at how long it's taken us to get to know and understand each other."

Ed continued to read the book, and it began to talk about what it means to love. After reading that section,

Ed began to think about his own ability to love and wrote down the question, "How can I love?" Before he spoke of it with Shelley, Ed took some time to ponder the question and try to answer.

How can I love better? he asked himself as he began his reflection. He thought about why he loved Shelley in the first place. *It's because I was attracted to her,* he thought. *It's because of her looks and something about her laughter that caught my attention. And when we finally spoke, she was so easy to talk to. She seemed to actually enjoy talking with me. It made me want to see her again and get to know her. And when I did get to know her, I simply found that I really liked her.*

But in the beginning, I just liked her. I didn't love her right away. So what was the difference? When did I fall in love with her? When did I start thinking about the possibility of marrying her? When did that seem like a wonderful idea to me—that I would want to spend my life with her?

Ed began to think more deeply about how he loved. *It's not so simple,* he thought. *It seems to go beyond how I felt about her, although that seems pretty important too. When I fell in love with her, it seemed to go beyond thoughts. There was something in me that felt deeply about her, who she was, and how easy it was for us to speak with each other, to share with each other what we were looking for in life. She seemed to fit all the things I was looking for in terms of wanting a wife and family. I felt lucky I had met someone like her and that I would be very lucky indeed if she wanted to marry me. I remember very clearly the night I proposed how nervous I was that she might say no; what would I do then? By that time I couldn't imagine life without her.*

Ed then began to think about the original question, "How can I love?" He wasn't thinking about it in terms of things one does to express love but rather in terms of how he could love at all. *What is it in me that caused me to love Shelley, to fall in love with her? What is it that makes us love? What is it that makes us respond positively to being loved? I think that's what I meant in asking the question. Is there even an answer to such a question?*

Ed then took his question to Shelley and shared with her his thoughts on how he loved her in the first place. He asked her how she understood love and how she saw her own love for him and the kids.

She thought for a bit and then answered, "I think I'm probably much like you. There was an attraction I felt toward you, and this grew after I got to know you. But you didn't quite fit into my image of whom I would fall in love with. I thought I would be looking for someone a little taller. It was an appearance difference. But as I got to know you more, inside you were closer to the man I hoped for. That made it possible for me to begin to give myself to you. I wanted someone I could trust, someone I could depend on when times got rough, someone who I thought could stick by his commitment to me.

"I would say that last point—commitment—was huge for me. There was no doubt in my mind that I would commit myself unequivocally to the man I loved, and it was essential for me to feel he would commit to our children and me. I didn't want to enter into anything I would think was unstable. Commitment, to me, was the very measure of a person's love. Less than that meant there was something other than love at play.

"I was so relieved to get the sense you were a person who would make such a commitment, and so when you asked me to marry you, I was relieved, because I was certain by then that I loved you and wanted to spend the rest of my life with you. When we were engaged, I felt the same joy as you did. It was wonderful; we had a future together where we could fully look forward to children, to building our family. It was you and me and them.

"And that's how it has worked out. Never have I ever doubted your commitment to us, and I love you all the more for that. I trust you utterly, and that's such a wonderful thing when you hear of so many stories of marriage breakup due to infidelity. I feel free to love you without reservation or hesitation. That's what it is: because of who you are, I am free to love you completely. I can't imagine that love could be better than that.

"I think that answers the question, 'How can I love?' I don't think I have another answer. When I think of the kids, that's what I understand my love for them to be. I am totally committed to them. Even when they get to an age where they can make mistakes in life, I will never turn on them or disown them or anything like that. I am here for them as long as I live. That's both how I feel and how I think. There is nothing I can imagine that would ever change that. I love them with all my heart and mind, and I can't think how that could possibly change. That's how I love. I am totally committed to them.

"And that's exactly how I think you feel. I can't imagine you ever turning against one of our kids. I knew this about you before we were engaged; I knew how you thought and felt about children. This was part of our being in sync with one another. I think we knew each other that well that we knew how each of us would be with our children. If this isn't a picture of our love, and how we love, I don't know what is."

Ed was very pleased with his discussion with Shelley. She knew exactly what love was, and she was able to put words to it that he was unable to. He agreed with everything she said, and he knew that commitment is such a large part of love. He realized this was the glue of love—the thing that gave love its strength through thick and thin.

Ed continued to read the book, and he found it amazing how his question dovetailed with what came next. The author dealt with some of these very same considerations Shelley had so clearly expressed. But now the book began to compare this understanding to an understanding of the love of God. He read the following:

> If we compare the love of God to the love between husband and wife, we see that many of the characteristics of the one are the same as the other. St. Paul says, "For I am certain of this: neither death nor life, no angel, no prince, nothing that exists, nothing still to come, not any power, or height or depth, nor any created thing, can ever come between us and the love of God made visible in Christ Jesus our Lord."[3] We can compare that directly to the commitment spouses have for one another and for their children. We must not make the mistake of classifying the love of God as something we can't understand. The whole essence of Jesus is to make the love

---

3 Romans 8:38–39.

> of God visible to us. It is Jesus who makes the love of God tangible to us. We can see his love for others in his life. We hear the love that is behind his words. Jesus is God's love embodied, God's love made flesh. Because of Jesus, we can relate to God in a human way. God became one of us so we could see, feel, understand, and enter into the love of God though our own feeling, understanding, imagination, and intuition.

Ed stopped at that point to reflect on the very things Shelley had said about her love for their children. *If God's love is like that for me,* Ed thought, *why wouldn't I want to be part of that? Surely that must be the meaning of the love of God—that God must want me to be part of it.*

The next day Ed read to Shelley what he had read the night before. "Doesn't that sound exactly like your love for the kids? Suppose it is true that God loves us exactly like that and is committed to us in the same way we are committed to the kids. Wouldn't we want to do something to find out how we can be part of that? I know I would, and if it's true, I would love for the two of us to try to find this out together."

Shelley couldn't get over the comparison of the description of God's love to her own love and felt that if God were like that, she would want to get to know him to see if he was indeed like that. "Yes, I'd like to try to find this out with you, because if God is like that, we owe it to ourselves and the kids to find out what that would mean to us individually and as a family. How do you think we could go about this?"

"Well,' said Ed, "Fr. Ben gave us the book, and he would be the one to go to. But first he asked me to finish the book before going back to him. So I think that's the next step—for you and me to finish the book, discussing it as we go, and then to go back and see Fr. Ben."

"Okay," replied Shelley.

She had no idea what a change in her life she was about to embark on, and not just her life but their life together.

Chapter 4

WHERE TO FIND LOVE?

The next part of the book began with a survey of where people try to find love and the things people do to compensate for the lack of love in their lives. It spoke of various addictions people have, whether food or drugs or alcohol. It spoke of various kinds of relationships we have that seek to compensate for loneliness or fear of actually committing to someone on a permanent basis. Mostly, though, it spoke of the effects of the absence of love in people's lives, and of the abuse that often accompanies this situation. It spoke of the effects of the behavior of those who have been abused themselves and how often their behavior was an attempt to save themselves from further abuse.

All of this led to a section on where one finds love. Before Ed proceeded with reading this part, he asked himself, *Where does one find love?* He recognized the truth of many of the things described up to that point and how people do seek some compensation when love is lacking. "But for people who have not found love in their lives, where would they seek it?" he asked.

He began to think about it in this way. He had a cousin, Alex, who had gotten into drugs when they were teenagers. In the end, Alex scrambled his brains to the point where he couldn't function in society. He couldn't progress in school, he couldn't hold down a job, and finally, he was placed in long-term care on constant medication to replace the drug of his addiction. He was permanently disfigured as a human being.

This was the most dramatic example Ed knew of personally of what the book had been speaking of. "But," asked Ed, "was the root of that the lack of love in his life? Or did that all begin simply in the search for some excitement or because of the influence of people he hung out with?"

Ed recalled what he knew about his cousin's life. His parents had been separated when he was a boy, and he grew up with his father. His father was always working to make ends meet, so the boy grew up in the care of babysitters and even from time to time with women his father was living with at the time. Then, when he was in his early teens, he hung around with a crowd that was pretty rough, and they were into petty crime. It was with them that he started using drugs, finally advancing—still in his teens—to the use of cocaine and heroin. This was when his erratic behavior began.

It was easy, after thinking about his cousin's life, for Ed to see that there was a lack of love in his life. It would be easy to conclude that Ed's cousin found friendship in the group he went with. He might have tried the drugs to find some excitement, but that didn't explain away the actual lack of love that seemed to have clearly existed in his life.

Would his life have turned out different if he had lived in a loving home? I can't help but think that it would have, Ed concluded. *In his case, where would he have found love? Surely it would have been in the home. That's where love begins, it seems to me,* Ed thought. *But where, given the circumstances of his upbringing, would he have found love? Did he find love in the friendship of his group? Clearly he must have found some friendship there. But did they love him into a better life? Cleary not. Did he love them into a better life? Did he ever meet anyone who truly loved him and tried to be a true friend to him? Where would he have found love?*

Ed continued to read, and the subject turned to some particular ways people try to compensate for the lack of love in their lives that are especially soul-destroying.

The first was the entry into loveless but sex-filled relationships where the whole focus is on the physical side of life. Ed read the following:

> This kind of relationship depends on the mutual satisfaction of physical desire and by its very nature, can last only as long as desire is satisfied. When this ceases to be the case, the relationship is basically ended.
>
> What happens here is that each person is divided in two, and one side is separated from the other. The person's body is

separated from his/her soul, and in this case, it is as though the soul doesn't matter. All that matters is the satisfaction of the physical. The result is that the soul dies a bit, or even a whole lot. This is because the soul is starved of that authentic love that feeds the soul, builds it up, and helps the person become the full person he/she is meant to be. Jesus said, "It is the spirit that gives life, the flesh has nothing to offer."[4] The soul has to do with spirit, and the spirit that most gives it life is love. Focusing on the physical feeds the body but not the soul.

When a person is given over to sexual desire, this can develop into a need that the body then comes to crave. When this happens, the other person is secondary to the need to be satisfied, and once satisfied, even if this takes some time, then the needy person can dump the other person because he or she was secondary from the beginning. The other person, in the meantime, having been used for this purpose, is left to deal with the aftermath of having been used.

But what does real love look like as compared to this? Doesn't the person who truly loves another place that person first before him or herself? Doesn't he/she seek the best for the other? Doesn't the level of selfishness in a person define immaturity in a person?

4 John 6:63.

> Immaturity is marked by the satisfaction of a personal need such as this and by using others for this purpose.

Ed reflected on these words and thought back on his own life to see the truth in them. He thought, *It was only after I married Shelley and began to identify what her needs were that I became aware that I had a role in meeting those needs. I think that is when I first realized what really coming to care for another meant. But it didn't happen before we were married; at that time, I didn't really understand these things. I was more concerned with my happiness, my life. I thought I could be happy with her. I wasn't as concerned as to whether she could be happy with me.*

The next morning Ed told Shelley what he had read and about his reflections.

"Well," she said, "it wasn't much different with me. I was more concerned with my own happiness too, and I thought I could be happy with you. I wanted to be happy with you. I think that's just where we, and maybe lots of people, were at before we were married. How could you have really gotten to know my needs and vice versa? This was to be part of the adventure of our journey together. I knew there was lots about you I didn't know, but I believed I knew you well enough to know who you were as a person. And I was right. My view of who you are as a person hasn't changed since before we were married. It's true I know more about your deeper needs as a person, but it's okay that I learned about these with time. What's more important, in my view, is that my love for you accepted that this would be part of our marriage and part of growth together.

"But as to people who have not known love in their lives—who in fact don't feel loved—I think we know many people who fit that description. But what can one do about that after the damage has been done? For such a person, can he or she find authentic love for him or herself without trying out all these different compensations? In other words, can one find the healing of one's heart for having lacked love in one's life?"

Ed answered, "I think that is exactly what this book is about. *Why Love?* is its title, and if I can guess a bit at what's coming, I think that love will be seen as the heart of the matter in people's lives. Maybe that's what I'm hoping it will arrive at."

The book continued with the story of a person who had been deprived of love in her life, and told of what became of her. Ed couldn't wait to hear this story because it seemed that was what was absolutely needed to give some sense of what can be done in a person's life. The story was this:

> Cathy was the third of four children born to Gord and Chelsea Hayes. Her parents had married young and found out soon enough they didn't really like each other, let alone love each other. As time passed, their relationship grew more strained, and the arrival of children into the family only led to Gord spending more time away from home, leaving Chelsea to carry the load of the children by herself. Her resentment of him grew with time, as did her resentment of the children themselves for being such a burden to her. As time passed, the children became more aware of how unwanted they were by both of their parents.

The effect on Cathy was multiple: she had very low self-esteem; she felt lonely much of the time; and she found herself spending much of her time by herself because her three brothers were off doing their own thing. At the bottom of things, Cathy never really felt loved.

She couldn't have articulated this had she been asked. It was a feeling that was ever present in her, but it was an unidentified thing. It did, however, affect how she acted in life, how she thought about things, and how she understood life itself.

Because she felt unloved, she came to believe she was unlovable and unwanted. The way she acted this out was to never really become friends with anyone, always fearing their ultimate rejection. She tried to be likeable as much as possible, but this too was aimed, finally, at not being rejected by others. As a consequence, she never voiced her own opinion on anything or let herself stand out in the crowd. When she spoke about herself, it was always in a self-deprecating way. "Oh," she would say, "I could never take on something like that."

She would never allow herself to be liked by a boy, and on the rare occasion when a boy tried to approach her, she would always find some way to not even enter a conversation.

Cathy became a very lonely, unhappy young woman.

Until one day when she was at university. She was away from home and happy about that. She had made the transition to university life, settling in to the routine of classes and study. One day she met another girl from her hometown and miracle of miracles, hit it off with her. In only a short time, they became good friends and then best friends. Cathy had someone to trust and talk with. They shared many interests, and Cathy found she enjoyed talking about how she felt about these and other things. Much of the talk centered on family and on being lonely within the family. Each of them shared that experience of life.

Cathy found she was becoming a bit more outgoing as a consequence of this friendship. Another girl became part of a threesome of friends, and this new friend had a boyfriend who Cathy liked immediately. She found she could simply be herself around the two of them. It was this young man who introduced Cathy to his friend Jim. This would be the first deep friendship with a man Cathy ever had. In Jim, Cathy met a man who was not like her father. Jim liked Cathy and enjoyed being with her. The two found they could talk about things that interested each of them. Each of them found they had a sense of humor that was enjoyed by the other.

They enjoyed dating when they had time available.

Cathy's first friend also began seeing a young man, and the now three couples found they also enjoyed each other's company. This was something like a liberation for Cathy. She had been freed from the shackles of how she had felt about herself. She now knew she could have friends and that having friends was a good thing. She now knew she could have a boyfriend and enjoy it. She found she really liked Jim and that she could be herself with him. She always felt at ease in his presence. She trusted him and felt secure with him. The thought that he could hurt her never crossed her mind. She knew him well enough that such an event was out of the picture.

The greatest thing that happened to Cathy as a consequence of these new friendships was that she was becoming more herself. She was freed from the imprisonment of negative feelings that had controlled how she responded to life and was able to meet others with a growing confidence in herself. Cathy was blooming as a person as a consequence of the love within these friendships. Some might think Cathy had become a new person, but what was actually happening was that Cathy was becoming the person she always would have been but for the lack of her parents' love.

> Such was the effect of lovelessness in Cathy's life, and such were the effects of love entering Cathy's life.
>
> Why love? Because it is love alone that completes a person's life—that makes maturing as a person fully possible and makes happiness in life a reality.

Ed was very impressed with Cathy's story, and he shared it with Shelley.

Ed said, "It just seems to make sense, and it makes the point so simply about the importance of love in one's life."

"What struck me," responded Shelley, "was that love was placed in the context of friendship and not of romantic love. To me, that's quite a distinction that you don't usually find today. I found it very believable, and when I think of my own experience of life, I can see that very same dynamic was at work. Good stuff."

"Good stuff indeed," replied Ed.

Chapter 5

ALL THE DETOURS AND DEAD ENDS

Just to move away from Ed and Shelley's story for a moment, it's worth taking the time to look further into the behavior of people and try to determine reasons for it.

If only people had a perfect understanding of life and its meaning right at the beginning, so much misery in life could be avoided. But that's not how God has made us. He has not made us free of misunderstanding, and these misunderstandings lead down so many detours and dead ends in life. How I wish I had known when I was a teenager what I've come to know over the years. But maybe some of this understanding can now benefit some of those who currently are living in the detours and dead ends of life.

It is the acquisition of right understanding that leads us out of these damaging paths in life. That being the case, all people are capable of coming out of whatever detrimental path they're on and moving into a life that is full—full of joy and meaning, purpose and direction. Right understanding is accessible and has wonderful consequences for those who will pursue it.

The key issue is this: what in life produces authentic happiness in a person and among people?

There are more ways in life to produce unhappiness than produce happiness. Jesus says, "Enter by the narrow gate, since the road that leads to perdition is wide and spacious; but it is a narrow gate and a hard road that leads to life, and only a few find it."[5]

Let us look at a few examples of the wide and spacious road that leads to final spiritual ruin—the actual loss of one's soul. The first example is very common in today's secular life. It is noninterest in things spiritual. This means that for these persons, the narrow gate to happiness is beyond their reach, even beyond the horizon of their awareness.

A man named George was typical of this direction in life. He had been raised in a family that had at best a lukewarm association with things spiritual, and when he was in his teens, he simply left all that behind. It wasn't even a decision he made but simply a way of life he drifted into. He had no idea what this would mean to him. There was no one in his life to warn him of what this could mean to his life and to all the decisions he would be making in life.

---

5 Matthew 7:13–14.

George went through university and became a research analyst in the field of microbiology. All his days were filled with experimentation, theorizing, explanation, and paper-writing. The more George became engrossed in his subjects, the more convinced he became that science could ultimately explain everything about life in terms of its physical properties and ways of doing things. He had no similar curiosity about why these things existed at all or where they fit into the larger scheme of creation itself. Because of his lack of interest in things spiritual, George's curiosity about physical things didn't prompt him to ask even the most basic of spiritual questions. This was compounded by the fact that most of his colleagues were of the same mindset. They too lacked interest in things spiritual: one could well say they reinforced each other's de facto atheism.

Even after George married and had children, his worldview and spiritual view remained the same. His wife shared his unbelief, and their children were raised in an environment of effective unbelief. So what did this mean to George, and how did it affect some of the decisions he made along the way?

One of the first simple but important decisions George made was where he wanted to live after he and his wife were married. He discussed this with his wife, but before that happened, he had thought it through and made up his mind. He (and later they) decided he wanted to move across the country because of a great work opportunity. This meant he and his wife would be separated from their past, their family and friends, and the places that were important to each of them in their growing up and in their memory formation.

It meant also the children were separated from the same things. It meant they would essentially grow up not knowing their grandparents, aunts, uncles, and cousins. Family for them would have a very limited meaning, with no essential history of coming together, of getting to love and be loved through time in a consistent manner.

From a spiritual point of view, this key experience of family love, which is one of our first and durable understandings of the nature of the love of God, was essentially missing from George's children's lives.

This decision, because it was made without any reference to God or the priorities of God, was made exclusively on the basis of career considerations.

But it was just one such decision.

Another decision George made, once they had completed their move, was with respect to the school the children would attend. Again, George didn't take much time to consider this. The factors considered were closeness to home and freedom from violence. As long as the school was deemed to be academically okay, then the school was fine with George and his wife. And so the children went to the school near them.

The fruit of the decision was that the children were further steeped in the effective atheism of their parents. What they learned in the school and through the friendships they made reinforced the belief system they were immersed in at home. They ended with no understanding of God, no inclination or curiosity about God, and developed friendships that were outside the orbit of God's influence.

The effect was that not only did that family have no idea of God, but they also had a diminished understanding of love that could inform them about the kind of love found in God. Each of the members of the family in effect lived each day without reference to God, and when the storms came, none had the rock that is God to count on or refer to. God was not only not the center of their lives; God was not even on the periphery of their lives.

When the children were in their teens, George and his wife began drifting apart. Soon they found they had very little in common. They had no common thing that joined them together at the core of their lives and acted as the unbreakable bond for them. Soon they decided to separate, and eventually they divorced. Even after they divorced, each of them sought someone, just as they had when had first met, who they liked, who they felt good being with, but with whom once again they would have no core bond that would see them through all of life's experience.

The children stayed with their mother. They continued in school and advanced from year to year. The effect of the marriage dissolution further impaired their understanding and experience of love. They simply didn't have a model of love they could actually believe in. Each of them came to the view that love was a "maybe" thing and you had to take whatever steps were necessary in order to safeguard yourself. Each of them, because of this thought process, ended up living in common-law relationships, none of which lasted. When each relationship ended, each of them re-entered another similar relationship. Two of them had children from one of the relationships that didn't last, and the children were brought up in an environment of unbelief, lack of commitment, and instability.

George, in the meantime, had lost his job when the company he worked for folded. He had a hard time finding the equivalent job he had and had to move elsewhere to get something close to what he had. He eventually lost most of his contact with his children and grandchildren. Even so, George's curiosity about the meaning of life, the meaning of marriage, and the meaning of covenant remained nonexistent. He never made the connection between how his life had unfolded with the meaning of life, marriage, and covenant. Indeed, the term *covenant* was one he didn't know. Life for George was a transitory affair that had no central point of reference. His life and his family's lives were reflections of this way of living. There was no rudder to the ship.

Let us now look at Andy, who is another example of how things can go badly in life. But Andy's story was quite different from George, although the outcome was similar.

Andy was raised in a family where his mother had strong faith and tried to live by it daily. His father was a believer but one who could be termed as weak. He prayed in emergencies only, never went to mass with his wife, and generally conducted his life pretty much as everyone else did. People who knew him could never have identified him as a Christian by the way he led his life. He was a good man who never did anything hugely wrong, but he was not a man led by faith or commitment to Christ, as his wife was. Anyone who knew her knew she was a Christian—a person who believed in Christ, was a follower of his, and practiced her faith daily. She was a visible Christian.

Even though Andy's mother prayed for her children daily, Andy showed a rebellious streak very early, and this characteristic of his personality became very expressive in his teens. When he was fifteen, he left home and went to a distant city, never calling home or his friends. He simply disappeared one day, and no one knew what happened to him; no one knew if he was dead or alive.

Of course, this caused great worry and distress for his family, especially his mother. She went to mass daily to pray for his safety and that he might contact them to let them know he was well. It was about six months later that the police in that city called to say they had Andy in custody. He had been picked up on vagrancy charges. He had no money and no job and was living on the street. This is where he was found one cold night and brought in out of the cold. Living on the street was illegal in that city and thus the vagrancy charge against him.

Andy's parents were relieved to know where he was and that he was safe. But why had he left like that? Why had he caused them so much worry? Why had he exposed himself to so much risk? What had they done to cause him to act in such a way?

Andy's mother and father flew to that city and brought him home. He told them he was restless and wanted some excitement in his life. He had heard certain friends of his had gone to that city and found it the most exciting place they had ever been in. He wasn't doing well at school, and so he had decided to simply leave all that behind and go and find an exciting life in that city. But things didn't turn out the way he'd imagined. He could only get low-paying jobs, and people wouldn't hire him because he was so obviously a runaway kid. Everyone told him to go home where he belonged. But he didn't want to do that. He wanted to keep on trying for a life of his own—the exciting life he had dreamed of. Even coming home was not what he wanted, he told them. He didn't want to go back to school, and he didn't want to take up with his old friends again. Mostly he didn't want to have to explain what had happened to him.

So the stage was set for this behavior to act itself out again. When he was nineteen, he again left for that city. But this time he told everyone what he was doing and promised his mother he would keep in touch. "This is something I have to do," he explained.

So he left, and this time he was able to get a job to support himself. He established friendships with some "cool dudes" and for a while he seemed to do okay. But the excitement he had been looking for finally arrived in the form of drugs, and before long Andy was into hard drugs that cost more than he was making. To support this lifestyle Andy became a male prostitute, and the degradation of his life was becoming complete. At no time did he let his parents know what was happening to him. At no time did he think to ask God for help, or anyone else, for that matter. In time Andy had impaired his brain through the drugs he was using, and the damage was irreversible. He lost his job and finally, though a series of arrests and psychological testing, was diagnosed as having drug-induced brain damage and was sent to an institution for long-term care.

Andy, driven by a desire for an exciting life, had destroyed his own life in an irreversible manner. He was now only twenty-six years old, and for all intents and purposes, the life he could have had was now not possible.

So what happened to Andy? What, ultimately, was behind his actions? How could a person who had common sense like everyone do this to himself—actually ruin his life? Does this not constitute the ultimate dead end?

Even though his mother had faith and prayed for her son constantly, Andy had placed himself outside of God's influence. He had no parameters by which to guide his own life, just the momentary and passing thoughts, feelings, or needs of the day. He had developed no overarching purpose in his life that led him day by day. He had never encountered God in his life at a personal level, and his curiosity about God was nil, so it could not have the dynamic that might lead him to God and seek his help. At the spiritual level—the life-with-God level—Andy had no relationship with God that could have saved him from his own inclinations that ultimately led to the destruction of his life as a full human being.

At the social level, Andy tended to form friendships with those who were like himself: dissatisfied with school and life itself. They tried to find interest in things that amused or excited them. This became a pattern of behavior in his life that he never broke out of or grew out of. In this Andy remained immature as a person, and this immaturity helped lead to his demise.

At the psychological level, Andy remained aloof from the love of his parents. The reason for this was that at a very early age, he was ill and had to be separated from them for an extended period of time. During this time, those who were charged with his care subjected him to some unloving attitudes and behavior. Without his own awareness or his parents' knowledge, he felt betrayed by his parents and unable to really trust or accept their love thereafter. It was a condition of his heart that was in need of healing that was invisible to himself and others.

The needed healing was never to come for him. Even the opportunity for such healing never arose. Instead, Andy's behavior was primarily rooted in this wound in his heart brought on by that early childhood experience. He was in effect forever trying to assuage the need for love in his life that was blocked by this wound to his heart.

The combination of these various factors were behind the direction Andy took in life leading to the ultimate dead end he came to.

There are lots of dead ends in life and lots of reasons for coming to them. How can they be avoided?

Chapter 6

COULDN'T WE HAVE AVOIDED THE MISERY?

If only we all knew how to avoid the detours and dead ends in life—and early in life as well. Wouldn't life be so much better if we had such wisdom at an early age?

If only we knew better than to give up when things get tough and to find another group of friends when we are being led astray by groupthink and group friendship. If only we had the wisdom to know when others are leading us down paths that diminish us as human beings, be they political leaders or local charismatic people in our lives. If only we could know when our own passions are leading us into trouble. If only we could know when our own wrong understanding is doing the same.

Sometimes it isn't any of these things that get us off the road we could/should be traveling. Circumstances in life can do it—circumstances that were never within our control or even ability to influence. Natural disasters affect our lives; political turmoil abroad affects our lives when decisions are made that affect us. Human illness has a huge role to play in our lives and how we are able or unable to move freely into the future. It's hard to think how we could have avoided some of the misery these things bring about in our lives.

So it isn't about necessarily avoiding some of these things that prevents misery from coming into our lives. It's more about having an understanding of life that gives context to some of this misery and yields understanding that allows us to face life with equanimity. And even joy.

The problem is this: this kind of understanding requires us to experience the very things in life we think we should be avoiding to be happy. Life itself is a learning process that can't be avoided and indeed is essential in our growth as human beings. And the true wisdom of life that involves God really only acquires depth through the experience of even the most difficult things in life, and maybe especially the most difficult things in life.

There are two scenarios of life that yield quite different results. The first is to live life alone—that is, to live life without the love of others; the second is to live life within the love of others. To go through life without the support of others who love us, are rooting for us, and are there for us is to live life without the support needed to live life fully. Being fulfilled requires love, our human nature requires love, and living life without love is like a plant that has no nourishment and remains stunted in its growth.

But living life knowing one is loved and having others to love is living life the way it is meant to be. Love is unique to human beings, and love is the rock on which a healthy and happy life is grounded. When one loves and is loved, one can go through the vicissitudes of life generally uninjured by what takes place or comes our way. We have our own base for healing, for support, for good advice, for checking how we're doing, and for affirmation or correction. But most of all we come to know what it means to give of ourselves, which, in the final analysis, is the very definition of the meaning of love.

Take, for example, a normal household within which there is love. The mother and father love each other and show it in the way they treat each other. The children grow up taking for granted the love their parents have for each other, and they also grow up within the love of their parents for them. It is primarily from loving parents that the children learn how to love and be loved. They experience in their daily lives the support of people who actually do love them in word and deed, who support them day-in and day-out, who come to their aid as needed, who offer their presence and guiding influence through the stages of growth as human beings, and from whom they receive the wisdom that is included in love.

The unfortunate person who grows up outside a loving environment such as this misses out on all of the above and forever is in need of these very things in his or her life. When these are absent, people need to find a way to fill the hole that is left by the absence of love in their daily lives. This shows how fundamentally important love is in one's life and to one's growth as a mature and fulfilled human being.

This is true on the natural level. But what about the supernatural level—the level of life with or without God?

The results are very similar.

When one looks at a happy family—a family whose members love and support one another—even this is subject to things in life that can overwhelm. But they have the strength that comes from their love and support for one another. They can count on each other when times are rough. In addition to this kind of support, their love for one another actually helps each other in their growth as human beings. In a very real sense, they don't have a fundamental need in life to overcome something vital that is missing. Even so, their love is imperfect, their support sometimes falters, and sometimes they simply don't know what the need is or how to provide what is needed.

The factors family life provides are a good comparison to life with God, for life with God is never as an isolated individual. Life with God is meant to be communitarian, much as family life is. Life with God bears a strong resemblance to the dynamics found in family life. Just as in family life there is the love between the parents that has such a profound influence on the development of their children, so too does the love within God have such a profound influence on God's children. In baptism people become adopted children of God and share in the inner life that marks the very life of God. It is not a magical thing but an act of God himself in our lives when we are baptized. We enter into the very family life of God as his children.

Just as parents communicate their love to their children through gestures and words, so too does God communicate his love to his children through gestures and words. Just as children learn love from their parents, so too do God's children learn God's love from him. This is done through what they see God do and say. Just as parents' love for their children is an intimate thing, that is, something that is conveyed through actually knowing their children and loving them according to the children's real needs as individual human beings, so too does God love each of his children personally and individually. No one in the family of God is loved more than another, but each is loved perfectly by God, who knows each person individually. And just as parents seek to correct children when they need correction, so too does God provide correction to his children when they need correction.

Let's consider the love between the parents for a moment, and then let us compare that love to the love between God our Father and Jesus his Son.

The love between parents comes first from their commitment to one another. In that commitment, they each come to know they can trust the other with their deepest needs, thoughts, and feelings. They know that when times are tough, the other will be there with him/her. They have decided to share their lives together for the rest of their lives, and within this commitment they raise their children. The love between the parents actually strengthens with time because their commitment to love one another is tested through time and life experience. They "learn" how to love and support one another through all of life's experience, and the result is a love that is tested in fire and that grows stronger with the passage of time. Indeed, it is the tougher times in life that they share together that actually binds them closer together.

Parents who love each other can share everything with each other. Through this sharing, they reveal who they are to each other, and this growing knowledge of the other increases their love for one another. It is this dynamic that allows each to simply be in the presence of the other and to feel at home with them. They enjoy a quiet peace in each other's presence. And the wonderful things they share in life become a source of joy to each of them. Happiness is felt between them as a consequence of the trust they have in the other and of the peace and joy that is exclusive to their life together.

Even though we have limitations as human beings, love can be an enduring reality in our lives. Even when our humanness causes ruptures, we have the ability to forgive and be forgiven. Indeed, this quality is a must in any love relationship. It is the antidote to those times when we fail in our love, and failure in our love will happen.

When we look at what we know of the love between God our Father and Jesus his Son, we see that love is central to their relationship with one another. It is not how well the job got done, how clean Jesus kept his clothes, or how well he did in school. Jesus knew the Father loved him, without conditions or limitation. When Jesus entered into communion with his Father through prayer, he entered into an environment of complete trust in his Father, and a complete willingness to do his Father's will because of that trust. Jesus knew his Father's love for him, and he knew his own love for his Father. There was nothing that could come between the love they had for each other. Their love for one another was complete.

The primary difference between their love and our love is that their love was perfect, not subject to sin, whereas we in our humanness always have to deal with our own tendency to sin.

Jesus knew the Father so well that he knew his will, and indeed, Jesus loved the Father's will for him because he knew nothing was more perfect and to be trusted than the Father's will. Sometimes, even when we love one another as much as humans can, our wills conflict with one another, and many times we have battles over our respective wills. So much human conflict comes from a battle of wills. No such battle existed between Jesus and his Father. They were on the same page in all they did.

When God is in our lives and we let him have his way, that same love that exists between Father and Son is lavished on us. God our Father loves us as his own, Jesus loves us as his own, and they come and make their home in us.

But we have our own wills and our own limitations in understanding and faith. Nonetheless, it is these very things we gradually learn how to yield to the Father, to Jesus, and to the working of their Spirit within us. Indeed, it is the nature of this tension that is the teaching ground upon which we come to know God in a most personal way and through which we come to trust and love God more and more. We come to know how much God is so personally connected to us, how much he knows the details of our lives, and how much he is at work in us in the midst of our daily affairs.

Remember the story of Andy—of how the early experience of separation from his parents so affected his life and how he sought to replace the loss of the love of his parents with pleasure or excitement? Let's revisit Andy's story at the point where he was in the distant city at age nineteen. There was a point after he had gotten into drugs, but before he had started on the hard drugs, where Andy had a chance to turn his life around, but he ignored it.

At this point he had a job, and one of the people he worked with, Bob, became concerned about some erratic behavior Andy had begun to display. One day Bob took Andy aside to express his concern.

"Look, Andy," he began, "what's going on with you? Something has changed since you first started here, and I can't quite put my finger on it. Are you in some kind of trouble? Do you owe money or something? Is there something I can help you with?"

"No," replied Andy, "there's nothing wrong. I've gotten in a little over my head, but it's nothing I can't handle."

The truth was that Andy had gotten into being a drug dealer to pay off some drug debts he had. Indeed, it was this that would eventually lead Andy into the harder drugs. But at this point, he was pushing the softer drugs.

"Listen," Bob said, "this is a tough town, and a guy can get into some pretty heavy stuff real quick around here. I know. I've been there, and let me tell you that it can lead you to some dead ends. So if you're into stuff you shouldn't be into, let me advise you to change all that right now. I can help you if you'd like."

"What kind of stuff are you talking about?" asked Andy.

"Drugs," said Bob.

"What do you know about drugs?" asked Andy.

"Look, when I first came here, I had a hard time finding a job. I was just like you. I had left home and came here looking for my own life. I didn't know anyone here, just like you. Because I needed some money I started peddling some drugs. I never used them myself, but I sold them to others and even helped others to get hooked. Pretty soon I found that I was part of a lifestyle that led nowhere. It's not what I wanted to be in life. I was lucky that I found a job here and was able to leave all that drug stuff behind.

"But there was something else that was really bothering me. Do you have any faith?"

Andy answered, "Do you mean religious stuff?"

Bob said, "Yes, belief in God, belief in Christ."

"No," answered Andy, "that all seemed like so much nonsense to me, so I never thought about God or things like that."

"Well, for me it was different," said Bob. "When I was a kid, I was an alter server, and I did believe in God and in Christ. My family had faith and brought me up in the faith. I still believe, and my faith is a big part of my life. So when I started getting into that drug stuff, I felt very guilty for what I was doing to other people's lives and to my own. That wasn't what I wanted in life. I wanted a normal life filled with family and happiness, and I felt that I couldn't be happy in life without faith and without Christ in my life. So part of my reason for dropping all that stuff was because I wanted a true life, with hope for happiness that included getting married and having a family. I didn't want to spend my life in something that was essentially meaningless. That was the real reason I gave that up. And if you're in that kind of boat, I just say give it up. Find out what you really want in life, and start working toward it. And if you have any faith background at all, I urge you to get right with God as your first step, and everything else will follow from that."

It was this simple conversation with Bob that helped Andy turn his life around. The first thing he did after work that day was to find a church he could visit. It was on that visit that he really prayed for the first time, asking God to help him sort out his life and set him on a solid path. As a consequence, Andy returned to his hometown, took up life again with his family, learned about faith from his mother, and even influenced his father to take faith seriously. Andy eventually got a good job and met a woman, who he later married, and they had three children.

Andy had found happiness in life and not a dead end. He no longer sought excitement or phony pleasures. Andy had put his life on a sure foundation. He never forgot Bob, and a few years later, Andy, his wife, and his family went to visit Bob and his family. They shared how that one conversation had led to Andy's thinking about his life and the direction it had taken. It resulted in Andy's decision to change his life and get away from the dead end he was living.

Chapter 7

LOOKING STRAIGHT INTO THE LIGHT

It's hard to look straight into a light. We get blinded first and may feel a sharp pain as our eyes try to adjust. If it were the sun we looked straight into, we'd likely suffer some permanent eye injury. And why would we want to look straight into a light in the first place when these would likely be the results?

But when we're talking about looking into the light of God, we're talking about something God has made possible for us. Scripture tells us that no one can look at God and live,[6] so God had to provide a Light we could see clearly and in such a way that would be to our ultimate good and not harm us.

6 Exodus 33:20.

> All that came to be had life in him, and that life was the light of men, a light that shines in the dark, a light the darkness could not overpower. The Word was the true light that enlightens all men.[7]

Jesus is the Light of the world, and darkness cannot overcome him. This is the Light to be looked at intently, and the more we look straight into that Light, the more will we find life—true, abundant life—and true happiness. "I have come so that they may have life and have it to the full."[8]

Do we believe this? Or do we say, "Oh yeah, sure," and then move on, never really appreciating the promise in Jesus' words? If we would just take the time to consider what he is saying …

It is life to its full, life in abundance, life full of peace, joy, assurance, and safekeeping. In the life Jesus speaks of, because it is life with him, there is nothing that can harm us in the sense of our soul. We are in God's safekeeping. We could not put our lives into better hands, could not seek direction from a better source, and could not place our trust in a surer mind and heart.

Where can we begin to look straight into the Light? Let us begin with Jesus' statement, "Come to me all you who labor and are overburdened, and I will give you rest."[9] He follows this statement with, "Shoulder my yoke and learn from me, for I am gentle and humble in heart, and you

---

7 John 1:5, 9.

8 John 10:10.

9 Matthew 11:28.

will find rest for your souls. Yes, my yoke is easy and my burden light."[10]

Could we have a gentler invitation or a greater promise of help? Jesus is telling us he has the power to do this for us—to actually help us with our overburden. He compares this to his burden, which he describes as light. "Shoulder my yoke and learn from me, for I am gentle and humble in heart." The yoke is what two oxen share as they pull their burden, the yoke distributing the weight between the two. Jesus is telling us he will share our weight with us if we will co-yoke ourselves with him. His burden is light, and he will take on half of our heavy burden if we will share in his light burden.

But how does he do this? How does he share our burdens? How does he make our burden lighter? Here is a story to give an example of how he does it.

Jesse was twenty-two when this took place. She had finished her education and had started her career. Her workload was heavy and her work hours long. In the midst of this, her mother became terminally ill, and she spent as much time as possible taking care of her mother. After some time, she found she was becoming exhausted, emotionally and physically. She felt something had to give, and she considered quitting her job so she could take care of her mother full time.

It was a great dilemma for her because she had landed the job of her dreams. It was exactly what she had been looking for with a company she had hoped to work for. Everything had been going so well for her, and she felt she was off to a great start in her career. She felt that if she

10 Matthew 11:29–30.

quit, she might never have another chance to work for that company. She did not have enough time with the company to request an indefinite leave of absence.

Jesse had faith, as did her family. They faced her mother's illness with great trust in God.

One night, Jesse brought her fatigue and her dilemma to Jesus in prayer. Her first thought was to remember what Jesus had said about the overburdened coming to him and he would give them rest. She needed not only physical rest but also a resolution to her dilemma that would bring her peace. Jesse had great faith in Jesus and total trust in him because she knew he was constantly with her.

"Jesus," she said, "you know how tired I am and what a pickle I'm in with work and mom. Help me, Lord, to sort all this out. I know you will help me. I need to know what I should do. Should I quit? If I don't quit, I don't know how long I can carry on taking care of mom. I just seem to be between a rock and a hard spot, and none of the options seem very good. Help me, Lord, to know what to do."

She sat quietly, consciously placing herself in Jesus' care. She knew she couldn't do a better thing than what she was doing right now, that she couldn't bring her problem to a better person. With this confidence she awaited Jesus' response.

It didn't take long. The first thing that happened was that Jesse imagined that Jesus came and sat beside her. He took her hand and just sat quietly with her. She could feel the reassurance of his presence, and she felt the worry start to dissipate. She began to relax in his presence, and she felt that he was indeed going to help her.

As they sat together, Jesus wrote something on Jesse's hand. At first she couldn't make out what it was, but then she slowly began to see what it said. When she saw what it was, she began to cry. She knew that Jesus had provided the perfect resolution to her problem, and she wept in gratitude for what he had just done for her. Once again Jesus had provided her with direction for her life.

The message was this: "First things first."

When she opened her eyes, she looked at her hand to see what was written, and of course, there was nothing. She had seen it in her prayer, and she immediately knew the meaning. She had already put God first by coming to Jesus with her need. But now the message from Jesus was clear. Her mother, of course, came first in her love and her time. Her work was not to be disregarded, but it came second to her mother. She decided to explain her situation to her boss and hope she could find a way to resolve her dilemma.

Indeed, her boss totally understood Jesse's predicament and arranged for Jesse to have whatever time she needed to care for her mother. The company even offered to provide some nursing care for Jesse's mother, and this turned out to be a great help to her mother and to Jesse. Her mother would die four months later, and Jesse was able to spend all of the last week with her. Jesse had never experienced the level of the love the two shared in that week, and neither of them had ever experienced so much spiritual consolation as they did during that time. Her mother received the sacraments of the church in the midst of her family, and all were at peace as the end came.

Jesse couldn't think of what else could have been done for her mother, and she was so grateful to her company for understanding her need and responding to it. This formed a true bond between her, her boss, and the company that would last. All had been done perfectly, and Jesse never forgot her prayer to Jesus and the perfection of his response.

This was a perfect example of the light of Christ at work in a life and how he shared the burden of his follower. It wasn't just any sharing of that burden; it was the perfect sharing of that burden. The light of Christ had again come into the world in the lives of everyday people.

One can look at the light of Christ from any number of angles, but one particular angle is most telling of the nature of Christ and how he takes "away the sins of the world."[11]

Light permits us to see, and it illuminates what is in the darkness. To see how Christ takes away the sins of the world, we need to see clearly the nature of sin and its darkness.

The darkness of the soul can be black indeed, and such was the case with Eddie, a young man who had given himself over to the powers of darkness. Light could barely make its way into that darkness, so closed off from the light it had become.

It wasn't always this way with Eddie. It's more like something that began small and grew into a weed that was strangling all the goodness that was in Eddie. His thought process was completely skewed in a certain direction to the point that he was closed to other thought processes. His

---

11 Communion Rite of the Mass, invocation at the breaking of the consecrated Bread: "Lamb of God, you take away the sins of the world, have mercy on us."

feelings were completely buried behind a wall of toughness needed to survive in the world he inhabited, and his spirit was closed to love and hope. Spiritual matters were not even on the horizon in Eddie's world.

When Eddie was a little boy, his father died. Later, his mother developed a serious illness that institutionalized her for several years. He was sent off to another city to live with an aunt who was willing to raise him but who had no particular love for Eddie and actually harbored resentment for having to take care of him. Nothing was ever said about this, but Eddie felt the lack of love and his aunt's resentment.

As Eddie grew older and had more opportunities, he spent more and more time away from his home, staying at friends' homes when he could. This was just fine with his aunt; the more he was away, the less she had to be concerned about him. Indeed, she was absent more and more from her home as she carried on her social life. Eddie was an impediment to her life, and she welcomed his absence.

Eddie was only nine when he first began to smoke. He stole money so he could buy cigarettes. He had no interest in school and was moved from grade to grade in spite of failing marks. After a while, even his teachers stopped trying to get him interested in school. They couldn't put their finger on what it was that would interest Eddie or what would motivate him toward developing his own life.

For Eddie, life wasn't a good thing. If he ever considered life—which he didn't—he would have said it was a grind, with no happiness. The best he could do was to make each day bearable. The way he did this was by developing friendships with those who shared his gloomy assessment of life, and together they tried to find ways to put something interesting into the day. They usually did this by stealing and trying to get away with things they shouldn't do. It was a kind of game for them to see how they could outwit people. This was a well-entrenched behavior pattern by the time they were eleven years old.

Doing "good" was seen as a sissy thing to do. The cool thing to do was to be tough and be seen to be tough. The best thing one could do, even with people who were older and tougher, was to let it be known that in some way Eddie and his friends would get even if someone got in their way. This proved a good strategy when a sixteen-year-old beat up someone in Eddie's gang. Eddie and his friends hunted the sixteen-year-old down one night and stabbed him several times, with the intent of killing him. It was only because of luck that he survived, and when he did, he refused to name who had attacked him out of fear of these young thugs. He knew they would kill him the next time, and most assuredly they would have. The word went out that these kids were all they said about themselves: they were ruthless, acting without conscience, and capable of doing the cruelest acts.

Eddie had a chance to think about his life when one of his gang friends decided he'd had enough and that he wanted a different future. One night he told Eddie he'd gone to see a priest who was a third cousin of his seeking some understanding of what life was about. He had known some kids who had made it out of this lifestyle and had made a life for themselves.

One had recently come back to visit his family, and he met Eddie. He told Eddie he was married now and had two young sons. He said he had gone back to school and now had a good job that would provide for him and his family. He said that his wife was a person of faith who explained faith to him in ways he had never understood before, and that now he had faith too and was trying to live his life in that faith and, with his wife, bring his children up in a loving and faith-filled family environment. He encouraged Eddie to break with the dead-end life he was now leading and to try to get a life that had the possibility of real happiness in it.

Eddie's friend's priest cousin also tried to explain the purpose of life to him from a "God" point of view. But Eddie thought about his situation and concluded there was no way he could break out of his gang. There was no place for him to go, and by now he had failed so miserably at school that the idea of taking school seriously was, for him, out of the question. The idea of life with God didn't resonate in Eddie's heart; it was all just bafflegab to him.

Then there was the issue of breaking his dependency on drugs; that too seemed impossible for Eddie. And if he quit being a source of drugs to others, where would he get money to live on and buy his own drugs?

By the time Eddie was twenty-two, he was a wasted shell of a person. He had no real friends, and his drug addiction had long since progressed to hard drugs. His health wasn't good, nor was his psychological makeup. He had become a fearful person who always carried a gun. He was quick-tempered, and this combination made him a very dangerous person indeed. No one loved Eddie, and Eddie loved no one. Love wasn't a part of his daily life. Mere survival was.

One day, in a fit of temper, Eddie killed another member of the gang. In retaliation, the gang hunted Eddie down and killed him. They took their time to make sure he suffered. Eddie died feeling their hatred for him.

The darkness of the soul can be black indeed. The light of Christ never gained entrance to Eddie's soul, and it was the light of Christ that could have saved Eddie from his sin. Eddie was the captive of sin, and he lived and died in that captivity.

Had Eddie emulated his friend who broke away from the gang and found life in Christ, he would have discovered the nature of sin and what the light of Christ does. He would have discovered that Christ wanted to be in his life and to be his Savior and his friend. The light of Christ would have revealed the love of God for him and to him, and he would have found that living in this love is the very foundation for true happiness in life, now and forever.

Eddie would have been freed from the captivity that ultimately killed him. Before Eddie died at the hands of his fellow gang members, he was already dead in his soul. The life of God that frees us had no access to Eddie's soul, and even when Eddie had the chance to choose another life and take the risks needed to move in that direction, he chose death instead. Eddie never really understood what it was he was choosing, but this didn't alter the effect of his decision.

What was the nature of Eddie's sin?

Sin is what diminishes life and in particular life with God. Sin separates us from God, and ultimate sin separates us from God entirely. The love of God saves us from that separation when we enter into life with him. Eddie's life totally precluded him from life with God and the love of God for him. Eddie never learned what life was about, how to live it, or how to mature as a person. In time Eddie's humanity had shriveled to a point where he was neither able to give to others or to receive what was good from them. Eddie's humanity was dead. Eddie's soul was dead.

"I have come so that they may have life and have it to the full."[12] Eddie knew nothing of this life that Jesus brings.

---

12 John 10:10.

Chapter 8

LOVE BEFORE AND LOVE AFTER

What happened to Eddie's soul after he died is a matter of the mercy of God. It is what could have been for Eddie during his life that is of interest here. Eddie, in and through Christ, could have been saved from the life he had. He could have discovered the love of God for him personally, and the experience of this love for him would have had the power to save him and change the whole course of his life. That is what his friend (and it can be added, his *true* friend) was trying to tell him.

What could Eddie's life have been like had he responded to his friend and tried Jesus the Christ? Let's rewrite the story from the point his friend spoke to him.

Eddie returned home and thought about what his friend told him. He could plainly see that his friend had found another life that seemed to bring him happiness.

But how can I do it? he asked himself. *How can I leave here and find another life like he did? What would I do for a living? How can I shake the drugs? Will the gang come after me if I leave? And if I stay here, surely they will treat me as a traitor.*

He couldn't imagine how he could do it, but he thought it was at least worth a try. He decided to seek the advice of a priest the next day.

He found the pastor of the church in his neighborhood at home and met with him. He told Fr. Ernesto about his life, about his friend, and about his dilemma.

"Father," he said, "how could it be possible? I can't leave here. I have no place to go, no relatives elsewhere where I could go to live. If I stay here, I think someone would end up trying to kill me. And then the drugs—I've been hooked for so long, I don't think I can do without them. I think I'd like to have a new life, but I can't even imagine what a new life would look like. I don't really have any education to speak of. How could I go back to school at my age? I'd look like an idiot in front of all those kids. And a lot of the kids around here think I'm the cool dude. What would they think of me then? I'm the tough guy; they respect me. And if they don't—well, they knew that could cost them. If I became religious or something, they'll think I've gone soft. They're not gonna think so good of me. What'ya think, Father? Any hope for a kid like me?"

Father looked at him with caring and asked, "What would life be like if we had no hope, Eddie? Sure there's hope for you. Why not? It may not be easy, but there is hope. The very fact that you came to me shows there's a desire in you for something more—something better—in your life. But let's start with first things. Did you ever believe in Jesus, Eddie?"

"Naw," said Eddie. "I've always thought that was for sissies. But my mother believes in him. In fact, I think she always prays for me."

"No doubt about that, Eddie," said Father. "That's what mothers do who have faith and who love their children. Well, Eddie, this may surprise you, but faith in Jesus Christ is not for sissies; it's for real men. You have to have courage to be a Christian, Eddie, because lots of bad things can happen to a Christian simply because he is a Christian. Take the example of how people in your life may think of you if you become a Christian. They may mock you and ridicule you. Some of them may want to kill you if they think you have betrayed them. That's not so easy, is it? In fact, it may be a lot easier for you to not become a Christian, Eddie."

"Really, Father?" asked Eddie. "I never thought of it that way. And what you said is probably true. But if I became a Christian, what would it mean to me? Why would I want to?"

"Because God wants you to, Eddie. That's why."

"But Father, that doesn't mean anything to me."

"I know Eddie," replied Fr. Ernesto. "Look, Eddie, you're just a kid. You haven't really learned how to live properly yet. Where kids elsewhere have had a chance to grow up in more ordinary circumstances, you haven't had that chance. You've grown up surrounded by violence and crime. You don't know anything else. If you don't take this opportunity to change the direction of your life, you may never have another chance. You may just get deeper and deeper into this gang lifestyle, and one day it may even cost you your life. In the meantime, you won't give yourself a chance to develop your talents or find a job you'd like and want to do for a living. Right now all you know is how to steal. And to pay for what? Not a family you're trying to bring up but drugs that you think make you feel better. You don't know how to live this other life.

"Your friend decided he wanted out of this life that you are stuck in. He wanted to be free to make good choices in life and not to be captive to how he thinks others in the gang might think about him. Right now, what you don't realize is how truly captive to your lifestyle you are. But you've done a good thing by coming here, because now you have chance to think about your life and where it's going. You have a chance to choose another direction that will give you a life worth living.

"Jesus wants you to have true happiness in life, and this is what life with him is all about. It's about living your life free from the kinds of things that now keep you captive. What's in it for you? Freedom. New life. Happiness. Ability to mature as a human being. Ability to marry if you choose and have a family and be able to love them and be loved by them.

"All these kinds of things have been made out to be uncool to you by other kids who don't know what this other life is about either.

"So one of the first things you have to do is decide, as best you can, what you want out of life. Do you want to be a criminal all your life with no skills developed to do anything else? You're well on your way to being trapped in this life. And I can tell you the likely outcome of this life is an early death for you and never having really tasted what good life is.

"Or do you want to get out of that life and develop a life for yourself that involves love of others and the development of the ability to accept responsibilities in life?

"In order to decide this, there are a few things you need to know, and because you don't know this out of your own life experience, you are going to have to trust I'm telling you the truth. Why would I want to mislead you when you've come to me expecting to get some help? When you were little, you relied on your mother to tell you the truth about what to eat, what to wear, whom to trust, and whom not to trust. I'm asking you to rely on me now to tell you the truth.

"The first truth is this: God loves you. These three simple words are the key to living a truth-filled life. Without this knowledge, everyone flounders at how to live life. You have to believe me when I tell you that God knows you personally—better than you know yourself, better than anyone else knows you. He knows you and loves you and wants the best possible life for you, and God will help you get there. God made us to know and love him in this life. When we get to know God, we get to know how much he loves us and how much he wants to be part of our everyday lives. This is actually the secret to living a happy life.

"You are just fifteen years old, and normally fifteen-year-old kids can wait to find out this secret to life, but you are in desperate need to know God now because you need his help to steer your life from this moment on.

"The second truth you and all of us need to know is that love is the great secret to life. For love were we born, because God is love. God's love is so great that he created mankind so that we could share in his life. I know you won't understand all of this just yet, but as you grow into a man, you will come to understand all this. What this means is that we need to get to know how to love others and have others love us. The teacher who was looking for the best for you was an example of this love. Your mother is a wonderful example of this love. She sacrificed herself for you over and over again when you were born, when you were sick, when you needed a hug, and when you needed all kinds of help. We need other people, and other people need us. The friends you have in the gang are an example of how we need each other. The problem there is that they are pursuing a lifestyle that is self-destructive.

"The third thing you need to know is that there are people who will help you find your way in life: your mother will, I will, your teachers will, even the police will if they know you're trying to live a new life.

"So, Eddie, is any of this making any sense to you?"

"I think so, Father. I want to believe you. But how do I get over the drug addiction? How do I get into school? What do I do about the drug pushers?"

"Well," said Father, "let's begin by taking one step at a time. This doesn't all have to be done at once.

"The first step is for you to seek God's help, because you are going to need his help. The second step is to find a place for you to live where you can come off the drugs. This will be a safe place for you to be, Eddie, while you're doing this. The third step, once you're free of the drugs, is to get you back into school. When we get to that point, we can look into what's available for you. Are you willing to get started on this?"

"Yes, Father, I am," said Eddie. "Thanks for the help, Father."

"Good, Eddie. Now I want you to go home and stay there tonight. Then tomorrow morning I want you to come and see me for an hour. I want you to start getting to know God. Tonight I want you to say the Our Father with your mother. Will you do that, Eddie?"

"Yes, Father."

"Good. Now, just before you leave, I want to call your mother to tell her what you have decided to do and to ask her to help you."

That night, Eddie told his mother all about his conversation with Fr. Ernesto and why he went to see him in the first place. His mother was ecstatic at what had taken place and told Eddie she would do whatever she could to help him. She told him this was exactly the right thing for him to have done and that she was sure, with Father's help, that Eddie would find a new, safer, and happier life. They ended by praying the Our Father together, with his mother encouraging Eddie to place all in God's hands and to rely on God acting through Fr. Ernesto to guide him.

The next day Eddie returned to see Fr. Ernesto, who began with some good news.

"Eddie," he said, "I have the perfect place for you to go for your drug addiction. It is a place run by Catholic sisters, so you will be in a good Catholic environment. I know some of the sisters there, and I know you will be in good hands with them. They have long experience with drug-related problems and have helped many, many people to get free. They will take good care of you.

"Before you go there, I want to get you started in your own life with God so that you will know how to pray and how to listen for his voice. Mostly, though, I want you to know who God is and where you fit into God's world.

"Did you pray the Our Father with your mother last night?"

"Yes, Father," replied Eddie.

"Good, Eddie. That is the best way to pray, to God your Father. Begin today to think of God as your Father, for that he truly is. Eddie, this is the truth—God is your Father, the best Father you will ever have, and he made you to be his son. Think of yourself as God's son. This is who you actually are. You are God's beloved son, and as such you belong to the vast family of God who are his children.

"When you pray to your Father, not only think of yourself as his son but *feel* yourself as being his son. Then you can speak to God your Father about anything, and you can ask him anything. This is what prayer is. The best prayer in the world is the one Jesus taught us. It is Jesus who taught us to call God Father. Learn that prayer, Eddie, and pray it each day. Think about the words, and learn to pray them with meaning. Try to say them as though God your Father was sitting next to you. That's how close God is to you, Eddie, and if you pray this way, you will see how good prayer is.

"After you've prayed the Our Father, take some time to talk to God. Tell him how your day is going and what things may be troubling you. Tell him what you may be happy about. Tell him also about the people you're concerned about, and ask him to help them. If you can be of some help, offer to help in whatever way you can. This is the way, Eddie, to live your life daily with God your Father. Never think, Eddie, that God doesn't hear your prayer. Never think that God doesn't answer your prayer. Just let him answer it the way he wants, for he knows exactly what is best for you and for each person.

"The next person you need to get to know is Jesus. The most important thing you need to know about Jesus is that he lives now and is with you. When you turn your life over to Jesus, and that is what you need to do, he will take personal responsibility for you. He will come and live in you, and the only way you can be parted is if you do the parting. Jesus has put your life with him into your hands. Jesus is the guardian of your soul, and it is through Jesus that you will truly come to know who God is, because Jesus is God. When you hear the gospel at mass, you are hearing Jesus speak, and it is Jesus who truly teaches us what life is about. You need to learn how to hear him and to come to understand what he is saying.

"Last, you will come to know about the Holy Spirit, who is at work in you and others. It is through the Holy Spirit that God gets done what he wants done. It's the same with you. The more you turn to God, the more will the Holy Spirit be at work in you, because you are giving him permission to live and act in you.

"When you are with the sisters, I want you to go to mass every day. Ask them to teach you the mass so you know what is going on and what it means to you. This will be your daily way of giving yourself to God and for God to give himself to you.

"I know that you don't understand everything I've just said to you, but I want you to believe that everything I've said to you is true. You will discover this for yourself through your own experience with God as time goes on. You will come to know for yourself that God is always with you and how much he loves you. You may not believe this now, but you will actually come to love God, and when this happens, you will be able to love others better than you ever have, and you will be able to receive love from others, just as you have become able to be loved by God.

"Eddie, this is what life is all about. It is all about God's love. Even before any of us were born, God loved us. He created us out of love to share in his life and love. He created us to love and be loved. And after everything is over in this life, he created us to share in his love forever. And at that time, Eddie, there will be no more sorrow or tears or hardness of heart. Eddie, this is the life God wants you to have. And there is nothing except your own sin that can prevent this from happening to you. Eddie, trust God with your life now. He will never let you down. You wanted a new life, and you are going to be given the best life possible by God himself. Learn to know and follow him.

"I want to call your mom now and tell her we're coming over. I want to explain everything to her so that she knows what to expect, how long you'll be away, where she can reach you, and when she can visit you.

"You'll be leaving tomorrow. I'll be taking you myself. Are you okay with all this, Eddie?

"Yes, Father. Thank you."

Chapter 9

LOVE ENDURES

Eddie went to live with the sisters for three months, and by the end of his time there, several things had been accomplished: Eddie was free of drugs; Eddie had learned the mass and how to pray; and Eddie now knew how to trust God. He also knew what it was like to have people care for him and guide him properly. Eddie felt safe with the sisters and felt they really did want the best for him. He saw their own faith at work, how they prayed for him and with him, and how they trusted God all the time.

The hardest time, of course, was when he was going through withdrawal. But even this time was made easier by the knowledge the sisters had of how to handle this phase. Eddie found that it was during this time that he prayed the hardest, asking God to help him get over the drugs so he could live clean. Eddie learned how to listen to the Scriptures during mass and to listen to the priest's explanation. Even in this, the priests who served that place made sure they explained Scripture in a way Eddie, and the others there, could understand and apply to their lives.

For example, one day Eddie was feeling the pain of withdrawal and began to doubt whether he could carry on. He wanted to run away and find a fix for his pain. He wanted to feel good again and knew how easy it would be to find the stuff. But then he prayed, "Father, help me. Save me. Don't let me go back."

This was just before mass. One of the readings that day dealt with the power of God to heal the person possessed by demons. *That's me,* thought Eddie. *It's just like I'm possessed by something that has power over me. Jesus, deliver me just like you did that man. Please.*

The priest then spoke of that Scripture and said, "I think each of you who are here recovering from drug or alcohol addiction can relate strongly to that reading. But here's what I want you to pay particular attention to—not to the thing that possessed the person but to the love Jesus had for that man in freeing him of that possession. Jesus had the power to free the man, but before that he already loved that man and out of that love wanted him to be free. Isn't it exactly the same for each of us? Jesus wants us to be free of things that imprison or keep us captive. For each of you, it isn't just that the sisters know how to help you to become free, but it is also that Jesus is here with you helping you to become free.

"In your darkest hours, when the demon beckons you the most, turn to Jesus to deliver you from that temptation.

Recognize what is happening—that it is your body that is craving for the demon, and it is that craving that is the object of all that is going on here. Jesus is here—bring your need to him in the offertory at mass. Give it to him, and rely on him to help you through this. He is making your suffering part of his own sacrifice. He will come to you in communion to live within you. Jesus is here for you. Lean on him; call on him; trust him."

Eddie heard these words and said, "Jesus, I trust you; I need you. I come to you. Help me, Lord. Help me."

When Eddie returned to his room after mass, he found the craving had gone and that he was able to carry on. This would be a pattern that lasted several days, and each time Eddie asked Jesus to help, the response was always the same. The craving would leave, and Eddie would be able to carry on. After a while the craving would return and Eddie would turn to Jesus again. After a few weeks, the craving went away. All of this was possible because the type of drugs he had used had not yet damaged his brain.

When it became known that Eddie was treatable and he could recover from the drugs, plans began to be made for Eddie to enter a special school for kids like him. All of the children in that school had the need to catch up in school because their education had been interfered with by drugs and lifestyle. They would be permitted to enter the school only on strict conditions formally entered into. Any serious breach of these conditions meant they would have to leave the school, and re-entry would be possible only under the most unusual and exceptional condition, meaning that as a matter of course, once a person left this school, he could not come back. This placed a seriousness on achieving results in learning they never experienced in the regular school system.

Eddie was accepted into the school. It was a publicly funded institution, so Eddie's family was not faced with the burden of paying for it. Eddie was very serious about this opportunity to get back on track. He was about four grades behind in school, and the catch-up would take about two years under a full-year curriculum. At that point he would continue full time until he received his high school diploma, and this would allow him to take university entrance exams if his marks were good enough.

A whole new future had been opened up for Eddie. The best part was that this school was in another city, and Eddie was billeted with a local family during his stay at the school. These families knew the background of each student who stayed with them, and they were selected because of some knowledge and experience they had of such kids. The government paid the families to compensate them for the cost of having the kids live with them

Before he left, Eddie had another visit with Fr. Ernesto. They had a long talk together, during which Eddie told Father of his desire to succeed in school. He told Father he understood the unique chance he now had at life and that he didn't want to do anything that would jeopardize his chances.

Father asked Eddie, "What do you think is the most valuable thing that you have taken away from your stay with the sisters that will help you for the rest of your life?"

Eddie answered, "That's easy, Father. It's their love. No question about it—I have never seen such love in my life. The extra things they did to help me when I was really struggling, when I thought I wasn't going to make it. I will never forget each of them. I know each of them by name, and I know I will go back to visit them when I can. I can't get over that they do this willingly, freely, with such love and commitment. Naturally, I had to ask them why they did this. I asked Sister Teresa to explain her life to me. I'll never forget her answer, and I want what she said to me to guide me for the rest of my life. I saw in Sr. Teresa the very heart of happiness, an example of the fullest life I've ever seen. It's that she has left me with, an image of what fullness of life looks like.

"She told me that her whole life revolves around her love for God. She told me it wasn't always that way and that she had to learn how to love God. It began with a growing love she had for Jesus, and then it expanded to a love for God the Father. She said this wasn't anything she could have done on her own but was God's great gift to her. She described it as something that happened to her when God showed himself to her in a very special way that changed her life forever. After this happened, she asked God what he wanted her to do with her life, and it was through this that she was drawn to be a nun, and even after she became a nun, it was her superior who assigned her to that school. She told me it was because God had so led her life that she was so happy serving him in whatever way he wished.

"That's why I say that she is the complete example for how I want to lead my life. Just like her I want to know God better, I want to get to love God the way she does and to have God lead my life just like he has led hers.

"This has already affected me, because I came to know that it was God who had placed me in that place, that it was God who helped me get through it okay, and that it is God who is leading me to this next place. That's why I know I will do well there, because I want to do my best now. I've learned how God works through people like you and Sister Teresa, and in her own way, my mother. I want to be that for others as well. God will show me in due course how he wants me to serve him."

When Eddie arrived at the school, the principal welcomed the newcomers and told them of the special spirit that prevailed there. It was a spirit of new life, new opportunity, of one for all and all for one. "Be in this together," he invited, "because all of you have a special background and an even more special future. You have been accepted here because of your professed desire to get the most out of your stay here. We can tell you that we are committed to you and will help you in any way we can. Help each other. You will discover that all the students here are rooting for you and they will help you if you need help. All the seniors will help you if you find yourself in need of help. And when you get to be a senior, I think you will find that you too will want to help those who are just coming in, as you are."

The family Eddie was placed with was a Catholic family. It was the school's policy to try to accommodate each student's religious needs since the school itself was non-religious. It understood the place of faith in a person's life. It was the desire of the school that each student grow as a full human being, and this couldn't be done if their own faith was left aside. So Eddie joined into the life of that family, attending mass with them each week and participating in their family prayers.

Eddie entered into this whole new pattern of life eagerly, and he did well in his studies. When he needed help, one of the teachers would help him, or if he needed some tutorial help, one of the seniors would help him. Eddie came to love the whole school environment; it really was one for all and all for one. He developed some very close friends in this all-male school. (An equivalent all-female school had been established separately.) By the time Eddie was twenty-two—the time he died in his other life—he had graduated and won a scholarship to a university nearer to his home.

Eddie went on to become a doctor who fulfilled what he had said to Fr. Ernesto—that he wanted to help others. This is where God had led him. Eddie's faith had been fully developed. He understood and lived his faith each day. When he was an intern, he met his future wife. They were married and had four children. Eddie was in love and lived in that love each day. He often recalled what Fr. Ernesto had said to him when they first met: "Eddie, you're just a kid. You haven't learned how to live properly yet." Now he knew what Father meant. He knew who he was in relation to God; he was God's son, God's beloved. He knew who he was in terms of what God wanted him to be in life. And he knew who he was in terms of his ability to love others, especially his wife and his children, but also his patients and their families. Eddie went back often to his special school, as did other graduates, to be with the kids and encourage them, and to show them what was possible for kids like them.

Eddie came to know the cohering nature of love, of how love made sense of everything in life: made sense of God, of creation, of how he was to love, of who he was in God's eyes, of who everyone else was in God's eyes. When he looked back on his school days, what he remembered and cherished most was the love he learned there and how everyone was for everyone. He saw the same thing when he was with the sisters; they were for him. He couldn't think of a better image of God than in these two environments.

But it was from the family he billeted with all through the time he attended that school that Eddie actually learned his faith. There was a wonderful example given by the parents in the way they loved God and their three children; in the way the children knew their faith and respected and loved their parents; and in the spirit of love that prevailed in the home. Eddie found that he loved being there; he loved doing his studying there; and he loved the mealtimes they shared together. It didn't take long for Eddie to realize these people had come to love him and he them. By the time he left them, he felt he was their son, and the parents felt the same about him. Their children felt he was their brother, and he felt like they were his brother and sisters.

Eddie had never experienced such completeness of family life. And he brought these experiences and understanding into the way he loved his wife and children. He realized also how important such an experience was to how kids grow up or they can "mis-grow" if this is absent in their lives.

Eddie's story shows the difference between a life led without God and a life led by God; a life led outside the love of God and a life led within the love of God; and a life led outside the authentic love of others and for others and life lived within that love. In a small way, the way of reference to a single life, this exemplifies the kind of life possible when lived with God in his love. It is a life that has been experienced over the ages by countless millions of people. It is a life lived in union with Christ for the glory of the Father in the Holy Spirit. There is no other life like it. It stands alone as God's gift to us—God's intentional gift of his life to us, to be lived in this life and forever.

God is love.[13] This is the purest, surest, simplest, all-encompassing statement of *the truth*. God is love. How sweet the grace that is filled with his love; how wonderful the Son he sent to show us his love; and how sweet the Spirit that is his love in action within us. It is this love that makes life sweet, that explains the very purpose of life, that fills it with hope, and that leads it day by day. Only the love of God in all its wonder can do all this. How sweet is God, who can turn our lives into something we rejoice in, that fills our hearts with a joy found nowhere else. Apart from this love, life is smaller, even without consequence.

This is the love that turned Eddie's life around and saved him from the physical death that was inevitable for him. But long before this, Eddie was dead in his soul. As a person, he was dead. As a son, he was dead. This is what Christ was sent to save all of us from and to replace it with the one love that endures through all, no matter what circumstance life may bring.

God is love.

---

13 1 John 4:8.

Chapter 10

PATIENCE AND KINDNESS

Love is always patient and kind …[14]

We can have a hard time thinking of love as always patient and kind when we know that even though we love someone, we aren't always patient and kind. We know we are, after all, "only human." Even so, we know that even in our human ability to love, we can be patient and kind, and that when we are most loving, we are patient and kind.

The love spoken of here is the Father's love. "Yahweh is tender and compassionate, slow to anger, most loving; his indignation does not last for ever, his resentment lasts a short time only; he never treats us, never punishes us, as

14 1 Corinthians 13:4.

our guilt and our sins deserve."[15] Even God gets angry out of his love for us.

I think parents who love their children can relate to that. Any of us who have been angered or upset by something a child does knows that it is a fleeting anger, something that passes and that is subject to our love for that child. Our love resembles the Father's because we are like him in never punishing as some of these things deserve. Rather, we try to use the event as an occasion to teach the child about love and loving others, including ourselves. We teach them how to be sorry for what they've done, and they see what our forgiveness looks like—just like God.

What would love look like without some of these characteristics that mark what love is? Love is marked by the ability to look beyond an action to the one loved, the ability to forgive and forget, the ability to return soon to fully loving someone, the ability to recognize what is more important—the sin or the sinner. They say God has the shortest memory of anyone when it comes to forgetting sin that is forgiven.

Love "sees" the person and looks inside the person to what is wonderful and eternal. It sees potential rather than a momentary thing; it sees what can be in the person rather than what momentarily is. God sees what we can be when we are not mired in our sin. He sees even a way forward for us when we turn to him. These attributes of love can be seen mirrored in our own loving actions that seek what is best for a person.

Take the example of Eddie. Things weren't so good for Eddie when he first went to the sisters for drug

15 Psalm 103:8–10.

rehabilitation. Eddie was a punk, a loser, a hateful kind of kid. The sisters had seen his kind before. It was their ability to see what these children could be—rather than what they were when they arrived—that allowed them to have patience and kindness with Eddie, even in the face of aggression. Where others might have thrown Eddie out, the sisters knew enough to stick with him, to love him into something better, so to speak.

About the third day after Eddie arrived, he went berserk. He hadn't had his fix; he was starting to shake; and he couldn't think properly. All he wanted to do was escape from that place and find a fix. He would have paid anything, done anything, for it. The sisters were in his way, these "goody-goodies" he was now stuck with. He was throwing stuff all over the place when two of the sisters tried to constrain him. He lashed out at them, hitting one of them across the face and pushing another over a desk. Two male assistants came to their rescue and forcefully placed Eddie into a room that was locked. While they held him, he was injected with something to bring him under control. All the while, his language was foul and abusive.

The sisters had seen it all before. Some could not be helped because their drugs had permanently damaged them. Mercifully, Eddie had not quite reached that stage. He was getting close to it, though; another year or less on what he was using and his brain would have been damaged irreversibly, and Eddie would have been lost, just like others had been lost.

The sisters were prepared for this kind of violence. They usually had male assistance when someone went berserk like Eddie did, but they had to try to control Eddie immediately because he was in danger of attacking someone. The male assistance arrived only moments too late.

This was typical of the early stages of drug withdrawal. The sisters weren't upset with Eddie; indeed, they had expected this behavior from him. No, it wasn't this expected behavior that upset them. It was something that happened after he had been there for about two months that surprised and even shocked them. It was then that their love for Eddie overcame their upset with Eddie.

Eddie had become quite fond of one of the sisters, Sr. Peggy. She was one of the younger sisters, was quite a joker, and was one of the sisters given responsibility for Eddie's care. She was the one that Eddie would most confide in, and when he needed help, she would be the one he would invariably ask for.

By the time of this incident, Eddie was well past the physical drug withdrawal and was more into the psychological withdrawal. His understanding of life was at a child's level, and his understanding of how to deal with psychological turmoil was the same. For example, his way of dealing with anger was to either suppress it or beat someone up. Since he couldn't beat up the sisters, he would suppress his anger. The result was that he went about his daily routine mad at everything. People couldn't really speak to him without him responding rudely.

He was in such a state when Sr. Peggy came to him one day to ask him to do something for her. She felt that he was well enough that she could ask something of him. This was part of their care: to ask something of the patients to get them to start taking some responsibility for their affairs. She asked him if he would be willing to assist her with one of the group sessions they had from time to time. Specifically she asked him if he would be willing to be the moderator for one of the sessions. He said he would, and that was that.

When the session began, Eddie seemed capable enough to get the job done. But at one point, he verbally attacked one of the newer druggies, calling him a weakling and accusing him of lying to others about what an important part of a gang he was. Eddie called him a coward who'd never be able to make it through the program.

Sister Peggy intervened and told Eddie to stop. Eddie then turned on Sr. Peggy and accused her of trying to have sex with him. Sr. Peggy was mortified by the accusation. She shut down the session and told Eddie there would be consequences for what he had just done.

When she got to her room that night, Sr. Peggy felt deeply embarrassed by Eddie's accusation and asked herself if there was anything she had done that might have led Eddie to believe what he accused her of. She concluded nothing in her behavior could have led him to such a conclusion and that he had acted for other reasons. She determined to find out what they were.

At lunch the next day, she went and sat with Eddie and asked him why he had accused her of such a dreadful thing. He wouldn't answer.

"Eddie," she said, "you just lied about me, and you need to find out why you did that, for your sake as well as mine. You need to apologize to me in the next session for what you've done, because you've left people with a doubt now about me. This can't be left that way.

"The most important thing now for you is to understand why you did what you did, because you may do this again. You may have done it before. The question is this: why would you say such a bald-faced lie? Eddie, you're not going to advance here until you answer that question and make this right. I want you to think about that seriously until you come to the correct answer—not just any answer, but the correct answer. There is a reason you did it, and you need to discover it. If you need help with it, speak to one of the counselors. When you've discovered the reason, the next thing for you to do is to determine how you undo what you've done. Eddie, you must take responsibility for your actions, and this is the way to do it."

With this, Sr. Peggy left Eddie.

At first, Eddie was annoyed that Sr. Peggy had called him on what he had done. But then he began to think about it and asked himself, "Why did I do that? She's right—I have done this before, a few times. Why?"

Eddie decided to call Fr. Ernesto to tell him what happened and to seek his advice.

"Eddie," began Fr. Ernesto, "that's a terrible thing you did. Do you recognize what a terrible thing it is, or does this just not touch you at all?"

"Father," Eddie replied, "I guess it is awful what I did. I thought it was just a wise-guy thing to say, like telling others what a macho man I am."

"Eddie, do you know what a good person Sr. Peggy is? Do you not see what a prayerful, giving person she is? The last thing that would ever enter her mind is what you accused her of. Do you see that?"

"Yes, I do, Father," answered Eddie.

"Just look what she's trying to do for you," said Fr. Ernesto. "Even with what you did, she's still thinking of you, putting you first, and seeking what's best for you. She's dealing with what you did in the best way possible. That's the kind of person that you falsely accused, Eddie.

"Now, she's absolutely right to get you to try to understand why you did this. I'm not going to try to answer this for you. This is something you alone can do. What I can do is give you a way to try to answer the question. Here is a way: First, be very clear about what was false in what you said. Second, why did you say this about this particular person, Sr. Peggy? Did you have something against her? Third, why would you accuse her of wanting to have sex? And with you? Fourth, once you answer these questions, what should you do about this?

"Before you even try to answer these questions, you have to try to pray about this and ask Jesus to help you. You have to imagine that Jesus is sitting with you and that you're talking directly to him about this whole issue. Once you've done this, I want you to call me back and tell me what you've come to." With this Fr. Ernesto told Eddie he would pray for him until he found out the truth and knew what to do about it.

Eddie went to his room and began to think about what had taken place. Before he did anything, he prayed about the issue and asked Jesus to help him sort it all out.

He then began to think about times in the past when he had done similar things. He recalled a time when he was just eight years old. He had been with some friends who would later join him in the gang. At that time, they were trying to be tough like some of the gang members they knew. Being macho was the big thing—who was the toughest, who was the most feared, who was listened to, who was followed. There was one guy named Jack who was around fifteen. He was known to have killed someone, although no one knew who it was or when. It was just a rumor, but it was spread with such conviction as to its truth that everyone believed it. The result was that Jack was the most feared kid around. When he threatened people, they knew they were in for it. No one crossed Jack or made fun of him. Jack was soon the leader of the gang, and what he said was followed.

One day Jack met a member of another gang. Jack and five other gang members cornered this hapless guy. He was about thirteen and small for his age. Jack was a pretty hefty teenager and much taller than the thirteen-year-old. Jack called him some demeaning names and decided to make an example of him, so he got him to strip and walk down the street naked. All the while Jack ridiculed him as a weakling. After they had had their fun with him, Jack beat the kid and told him never to come back into their neighborhood.

Eddie and his friends had seen this and were impressed by Jack. From that moment, their favorite thing to do with others they didn't like was to ridicule them, so long as they didn't think they could be retaliated against. This became a habit for Eddie. He came to lie about others when he felt like ridiculing them or embarrassing them.

Eddie realized—when he remembered this and others incidents that followed—that he had found the origin of the behavior that led him to embarrass Sr. Peggy.

"But why did I do it to her?" he asked himself. "Why would I hurt her?" He began to think about some of the people he had ridiculed or hurt over the years, and he realized they were all weaker than him. And the girls he had hurt had all been hurt by some sexual reference or accusation he made of them. He had found the easiest way to hurt a girl was to accuse her of some sexual thing. He realized he had done the same thing with Sr. Peggy. Eddie now realized that he had developed a pattern of behavior that was linked to gang behavior and machismo.

"But why Sr. Peggy?" he asked himself again. He realized that by attacking Sr. Peggy, who was the staff leader in the session, the figure of authority, he was trying to make himself out to be the tough guy, the guy to be respected among the other males in the session. *I was trying to make myself look bigger by trying to make her look smaller,* he thought to himself.

Eddie felt that he had sorted it all out. He also knew he owed Sr. Peggy an apology and that he had to tell the group, when they came together again, that he had lied and falsely accused her. He also knew that he had to stop this behavior in the future, to cut it off now that he was aware of it.

The next day, Eddie called Fr. Ernesto and told him his thoughts. Fr. Ernesto agreed with him and told Eddie he thought he should do one more thing after he had spoken to Sr. Peggy and to the group. He should follow this by making a good confession, promising Jesus not to do this again.

This is exactly what Eddie did, and from that time, Eddie never repeated the behavior he had developed as a child.

Eddie thanked Sr. Peggy for what she had done for him. "Sister," he said, "you would have been right to have really punished me and hated me for what I did to you. But you didn't do that. Instead, you tried to get me to discover why I acted so terribly, and because of this, I was able to change something in my life that was so hurtful to people. You showed me how much you cared that I should become a better person. You were patient with me, and kind, and thoughtful. Because of this, you have changed my life."

Eddie never forgot what he had learned from Sr. Peggy. He never forgot her and the kind of person she was. One day he was reading that part of St. Paul that spoke of patience and kindness and realized that Sr. Peggy was all these things and that he wanted to be like her.

> Love is always patient and kind; it is never jealous; love is never boastful or conceited; it is never rude or selfish; it does not take offence, and is not resentful. Love takes no pleasure in other people's sins but delights in the truth; it is always ready to excuse, to trust, to hope, and to endure whatever comes.[16]

That was Sr. Peggy. That was love.

---

16 1 Corinthians 13:4–8.

Chapter 11

HOPE AND FAITH

Can you imagine life without hope? Hope is like an engine that keeps things running. Without hope, everything that makes life worthwhile loses a principal ingredient; hope is that special ingredient in life that gives life vigor. Without hope, people subsist in life at a level that merely gets by each day. Without hope, despair is close at hand.

Hope exists at different levels: I can hope my team wins; I can hope I meet the right girl; I can hope my children do well in life; I can hope that I get the next promotion or job; I can hope my candidate wins the election. Each of these hopes can be fostered with effort to bring about that result. Hope indeed generates effort on our behalf. Hope can be, and usually is, attached to our very goals in life.

All these kinds of hope are normal human hopes that exist with or without God. When this type of hope diminishes or disappears, there is no hope to supplant it if God does not exist in one's life. But when God is in one's life as a daily reality, there is no such thing as life without hope. Life with God brings its own intrinsic hope, for one has hope in God himself. It is a founded hope, a grounded hope that is true. Our hope in God is what God himself asks of us. To place our trust in God is, at its base, hope in God. When all earthly hopes go unrealized hope in God restores life and gives us a way forward.

In the case of God, trust and hope are so interwoven that one can barely separate one from the other. Love is of the essence in our relationship with God; faith in God gives rise to hope, and hope gives rise to an active daily life with God. Faith, hope, and love are interconnected dynamics in the life with God. The hope we have in God is of a different order than the ordinary hopes we have in life. These ordinary hopes in life may or may not come to pass, but the hope we have in God is a different kind of hope. Christian hope is infused into the soul by God, a gift of God by the Holy Spirit.

> Hope is the theological virtue by which we desire the kingdom of heaven and eternal life as our happiness, placing our trust in Christ's promises and relying not on our own strength, but on the help of the grace of the Holy Spirit.[17]

17 Catechism of the Catholic Church #1817.

> Let us hold fast the confession of our hope without wavering, for he who promised is faithful.[18]

> The virtue of hope responds to the aspiration to happiness which God has placed in the heart of every man; it takes up the hopes that inspire men's activities and purifies them so as to order them to the Kingdom of heaven; it keeps man from discouragement; it sustains him during times of abandonment; it opens up his heart in expectation of eternal beatitude. Buoyed up by hope, he is preserved from selfishness and led to the happiness that flows from charity. [19]

We hope in the God who has been revealed to us in Christ by the Holy Spirit. Because we have come to know the very nature of God through the Christian revelation, we have hope in a Father who loves us intimately, and we have hope in the life he offers us in Christ. This is a hope that cannot fail us, for it is hope that rests on the very promises of God himself.

But we need to see how this hope plays itself out in daily life in order to see the vital role it plays in each of our lives. For this we return to Eddie's story.

In the first story of Eddie, by the time he was murdered by gang members, Eddie actually had no hope in life. By this time, his brain had been damaged by drug abuse.

---

18 Hebrews 10:23.

19 Catechism of the Catholic Church #1818.

He had no possibility of escaping the gang lifestyle or the drug lifestyle. He was trapped in a life that had but one end—death. It would be death by drugs or death by gang. Eddie had no belief in anything that could lead his life to happiness. Eddie was truly a lost soul without the hope that could lead him out of the life he had. He had turned away from pleas for him to seek another life.

By contrast, the new Eddie who had responded to the desire for a new life, and through the help of many had found it, was filled with the kind of hope spoken of here.

It was hope that led Eddie to see Fr. Ernesto, but that wasn't the hope we're speaking of. He had hope that Fr. Ernesto might be able to help him, but that wasn't hope in God. Hope in God began for Eddie that night when he went home and prayed with his mother and later when he prayed by himself. This was hope in God—hope that God could help him. This hope was further engaged when Sr. Peggy challenged him to face his own behavior and take responsibility for it. When he had come through this successfully with the guidance of Fr. Ernesto, Eddie's hope now had substance to it. But when Eddie successfully went through the drug rehabilitation and high school, his faith in God had blossomed, and his hope in God had changed shape completely.

No longer did Eddie's hope in God rest in something God was doing for Eddie. It included that, of course, but the nature of the hope was in eternal life and what eternal life had come to mean to Eddie. Eddie now knew he was God's beloved son; he knew what it meant to be loved by God and to love God in return. He knew God was completely in his life moment by moment, day by day. He had come to know God because he had come to know

Jesus. Jesus revealed the Father to Eddie, and Eddie had come to live the life in God meant for each of us. Eddie was truly living the life in grace meant for us.

So what did hope look like now to Eddie? Hope now meant that Eddie could look forward to more of eternal life—that he could live more deeply with God his Father and Jesus, God's Son, in the Holy Spirit. Hope meant that he could look forward to the same for his wife and his children. Hope meant that Eddie lived his life as a doctor in the sure knowledge that God was with him, and hope meant that when Eddie faced any medical situation, he could trust that God would be with him. Hope meant that what Eddie could look forward today in his life with God would continue tomorrow and that ultimately his life with God would culminate in life everlasting in the very presence of God in the next life. This was not hope hoped for but was hope grounded in spiritual reality. Eddie could live his life in this kind of confidence in God.

This kind of hope has the nature of assurance. This is because it is an infused gift of God that comes from this life with God. Jesus had this kind of hope. It may seem strange that Jesus had hope when he was God and knew all things, but the kind of hope Jesus had was the kind of hope that comes from God. He knew exactly what the kingdom of God was and had the sure hope that the kingdom of God would grow in the hearts and minds and spirits of his followers and in the world. Jesus had the sure hope that his sacrifice would bear the fruit intended in the forgiveness of sin and the bringing of his people into union with the Father.

Jesus' disciples, after Pentecost, shared in this hope. Their hope was based on their knowledge of God and his purposes—on the very nature of God they had come to know individually and as a community. It was not a misplaced hope but a sure hope rooted in God himself, a hope given to them by God himself. It is a hope that is as sure as God himself.

What about faith? How is it different from hope? What did it look like in Eddie's life?

Faith is that mysterious action of God in our lives whereby our blindness to God is taken away and we are able to see him. It is God's wonderful gift to us. It is an active thing within us that brings us to cry out, "Abba, Father!" It is more than mere simple belief that God exists; it is dynamic because it causes us to live as sons and daughters of God in a daily, personal, felt relationship. It is by this faith we live each day and in which we encounter God each day. It is this faith, this gift of God, that allows us to accept with joy all that God has revealed about himself. Faith renders what could be merely intellectual into something heartfelt and deeply satisfying. This faith brings with it the rest St. Augustine speaks of.[20] Unlike hope, which looks to the future, faith recognizes and causes us to live in the kingdom of God that is present.

Faith is like a muscle that needs to be exercised. If it is not exercised it withers. Exercising our faith means trusting in God, praying to the God who loves me, participating in life-giving liturgies of Christ's church, and receiving the body, soul and divinity of our Lord regularly.

In Eddie's life, faith developed in tandem with hope. The things that led to his having hope in the Lord also developed his faith in the Lord. Eddie learned how to pray

---

20 "Our hearts are restless until they rest in Thee."

daily, learned how to be fully part of the mass, learned how to trust God with everything, and learned how to give his life to God. Eddie learned how to be led by God in the direction of his life and how to take the stuff of daily life to God for sorting out and clarification. Faith and hope became active ingredients in Eddie's daily life, and through these Eddie's life with God became fully alive.

Here is an example of how this worked in Eddie's life after he had become a doctor, a husband, and a father.

Eddie was now a father of three, and at the time of this incident, his children's ages ranged from three to eight. Eddie's wife also worked in medicine so that between work and the home, their lives were very busy each day. Eddie had become a surgeon and by this time had become known for his skill as such. He was well respected in the hospital where he served his patients.

One of his patients was a young boy aged eight—the same as his eldest son. The boy had been in a car accident and had his left arm torn off and his left leg severely crushed, and the left side of his torso had terrible body piercing injuries. Eddie was the surgeon on duty that night.

When he saw the boy, he wasn't sure that the boy could survive the terrible injuries he had. "Lord, help me," Eddie said, "and help this boy." Eddie quickly put together a plan and called in the surgical team necessary. The boy's arm could not be re-attached; the task was only to close the wound as quickly as possible. The leg was determined to be salvageable, and they repaired what they could immediately. The greatest threat to the boy's life was the wound in his side where a piece of glass had stuck deep into his body, barely missing his heart but cutting through some key parts of his body. These were bleeding, and they had to act quickly to open him up so they could remove the glass and glass splinters and stop the bleeding.

All of this they did successfully, but the boy was so weakened by the injuries and trauma that he was now in grave danger. Eddie told the boy's parents that his chances of survival were very low. It was now a wait-and-see situation. It would now be up to the boy's own body to survive.

Eddie got home at about four in the morning. His wife came to him as he sat in his living room going over what had taken place to see if anything more could be done. He had concluded that everything that could be done was done. He had been praying about all this when his wife joined him. He told her what had happened to the boy who was the same age as their son. "Frankly," he told her, "the boy will need a lot of God's help to survive."

"Then let's take the time to pray for him," answered his wife.

That's what they did. For the next half hour, the two of them prayed for the boy's recovery as though they were praying for their own son.

This wasn't unusual for them. This was how they handled everything in their lives. Everything was part of their life with God. In this instance, their prayer employed their faith and their hope. They utterly believed in God's presence and in his love for them. They believed in God's love for this boy, just as they knew how much God loved their own children. This was so much a part of their faith that it was simply instinctive for them to pray with the fervor they did. Their hope wasn't in the skill of the medical team or in the boy's healing power. Their hope was in God, that God could save that boy according to his will for the boy.

Eddie finally went to bed but was up again at nine to return to the hospital. When he arrived, he found the boy stabilized, with all signs indicating he was not in immediate danger. Part of the medical team met again to plan the next steps in treatment. The arm needed some further work to make it ready to receive a prosthetic arm when the time came. It was the leg that now needed major work on it to save it, but this would have to wait until the boy was strong enough to take the multiple operations that would be required. In the meantime, there was no evidence of any internal bleeding. Eddie said a further silent prayer for the boy and then went on with other patients.

After three days, it was clear the boy had survived and was recovering. Initial work then began on his leg.

Eddie, his wife, and their children included the boy in their prayers together. This was just part of their daily life together as a family. When the boy recovered, they were all happy and thanked God for what he had done.

Faith and hope go together; they are inseparable. Each serves an important role in our lives with God and gives vitality to life. Both are linked to God's imminent presence in our lives.

But in the end, it is love that is the glue. "In short, there are three things that last: faith, hope and love; and the greatest of these is love."[21]

---

21 1 Corinthians 13:13.

Chapter 12

BUT IN THE END, LOVE

Love is the be all and end all in terms of the meaning of life and of the very nature of God. God revealed as love[22] explains everything about why God created the universe in the first place and human beings with the natures they have. Humans alone have the capacity to share in the very life of God.

"God sent into the world his only Son so that we could have life through him." It wasn't the hills and plains, the trees and veggies, the rabbits and lions that were created to share in the very life of God through Jesus, his Son. It

22 1 John 4:8–10: "Anyone who fails to love can never have known God, because God is love. God's love for us was revealed when God sent into the world his only Son so that we could have life through him; this is the love I mean: not our love for God, but God's love for us when he sent his Son to be the sacrifice that takes our sins away."

was us in the very nature of our humanity. The human soul—the very essence of our humanity—alone has the God-given ability to enter into life with him. But the way of entering life with him is absolutely unique. It is nothing we can bring about through our own doing. God alone has provided the way, and it is through Jesus that the way is found—the narrow gate.[23]

Jesus is "the sacrifice that takes our sins away." If Jesus' sacrifice isn't viewed as the supreme act of love[24] that it is, then we can miss this central, visible act of God's love for us. The evidence of love is visible in the passion, death, and resurrection of our Lord but not so evident is the love displayed in how Christ takes away our sin. This is the here-and-now dimension of the way God's love works itself out in our lives once we have united our lives to Christ. When we become aware of God's saving grace in our lives, we become aware at the same time of the nature of God's love for us. The nature of that love is shown as concern for our freedom to love, and the saving action of Christ takes place as setting us free from those things in our lives that limit our freedom and ability to love. In short, Christ sets us free to love and to respond to love. It is God's own action to set us free from the effects of sin.

Stories in the gospel show that setting people free to live as sons and daughters of God is of the very essence of what Jesus came to do. We see it in the story of the paralytic who was set free to walk again, but only after

23 Matthew 7:14: "Enter by the narrow gate, for the road that leads to perdition is wide and spacious."

24 John 15:13: "A man can have no greater love than to lay down his life for his friends."

Jesus freed him of his sins by forgiving them.[25] We see it in the gratitude of the woman who washed Jesus' feet with her hair, so thankful was she that Jesus had saved her and freed her from her sin.[26] We see it in Jesus' response to the man dying next to him on the cross when he told him he would that day be with him in paradise.[27] We see it in his action to save the woman caught in adultery when he bid the person without sin to throw the first stone. "Neither do I condemn you. Go and sin no more,"[28] was all he said to her. We see it in abundance in the way Jesus met the woman at the well and how he changed her life by revealing to her who she was and who he was.[29]

We can see the saving power of Christ in Eddie's life too—a saving power that revealed itself to Eddie as the most wonderful and needed love for him. The love of God in Christ brought Eddie back to life again, and more than that, brought Eddie the abundant life Christ promised to those who live in his grace.[30]

Let us see what the love of God meant to Eddie.

The love of God first displayed itself to Eddie through Fr. Ernesto and Sr. Peggy. But Eddie never experienced the love of God for him directly until sometime in the year Eddie was sixteen. By this time, Eddie was in the special

---

25 Mark 2:1–12.

26 Luke 7:36–38, 44–50.

27 Luke 23:39–43.

28 John 8:11.

29 John 4:1–34, 39–42.

30 John 10:10: "I have come so that they may have life and have it to the full. I am the good shepherd: the good shepherd is one who lays down his life for his sheep."

school and was doing quite well in his studies. He was committed to taking advantage of this opportunity for a new life and had entered into what was, for him, a whole new routine in life of attending classes and studying at night.

One weekend Eddie went home to visit his mother and decided to call one of his old gang friends.

This friend knew what had become of Eddie but wasn't sure what all this meant for Eddie. He assumed Eddie was still in some way connected to drugs in order to get the money to make all this possible.

When they met, one of the pushers was with the friend, and the two of them tried to entice Eddie into taking some drugs. Eddie told them he had stopped all that and had a chance for a new life free of drugs and all that went with it.

Eddie's friend and the pusher weren't having any of it. "C'mon, Eddie, have some fun with us. What's the matter—become too good for us? Is that it, Eddie—you're too good for us? Become a goodie-goodie, have you, Eddie?"

Now their teasing was turning to anger.

"It's nothing like that, guys. Some great people have been helping me get away from that stuff. You know Fr. Ernesto, Jimmie? He's been helping me. I went to him to ask if he would help me, and he has. He sent me to a place where I could get off the drugs, and one particular person there was a great help to me. And I've done it—I'm free of the stuff now. Then Fr. Ernesto got me into this special school where I could catch up and even finish high school if I'm able. Look, if you want I could talk to Father to see if he can help you too. It'll give you a chance to have a regular life. That's what I was looking for."

Jimmie and the pusher said they weren't interested. But Jimmie was lying—he didn't want to say he was interested in front of the pusher, who he knew would have no interest in what Eddie was doing.

That night Jimmie came to see Eddie.

"Hey, man, I was kidding before. I am interested. Do you think Fr. Ernesto would help me too?"

So Eddie took Jimmie to see Fr. Ernesto the next day before he returned to school. But after Jimmie left that night Eddie prayed for him, that he might find his way out of that life, just as Eddie had. It was during this prayer that Eddie first felt the love of God for him directly.

Eddie had told his mother about Jimmie and asked her if they could pray together for him. His mother was only too glad to do so. They decided to pray the rosary for Jimmie, and when they got to the fourth luminous mystery—the transfiguration of Jesus—Eddie began to feel something he had never felt before. It was like he was one of the disciples present at the transfiguration. In his imagination, Eddie could visualize Jesus being surrounded by light, and Jesus himself became luminous. It was like Jesus was doing this for Eddie so that he could see who Jesus truly was. Eddie began to realize what this meant—that Jesus was truly who he said he was, the Son of God. It wasn't that Eddie merely saw the transfiguration of Jesus, but he felt it as well. Eddie felt Jesus' love for him.

This had a powerful effect on Eddie. Never before had he felt such love from anyone. What he saw in Fr. Ernesto and Sr. Peggy was magnified in what he saw and felt in Jesus. Eddie knew Jesus' love for him in the most personal way, and from that moment on, Eddie would relate to Jesus on that personal level. The experience changed his whole understanding of the meaning of the love of God. He knew what it meant deep within himself—that he was God's beloved. When anyone explained that God was love, Eddie knew exactly what it meant. He had experienced it for himself personally and in the most indelible way. The result was that Eddie loved Jesus and the Father in return.

While on their way to see Fr. Ernesto the next day, Eddie told Jimmie of his experience. "Jimmie," he said, "what I experienced is true. I know it's true, Jimmie. Please, while you're talking to Fr. Ernesto, ask him to help you find your faith. He'll help you—I know he will."

After Jimmie had seen Fr. Ernesto, he told Eddie all about their conversation. "Eddie, Father is going to help me just like he did you. He's going to make arrangements for me to go to the same place as you did, and if I do okay there, he said he will try to get me into the school you're going to. Also, I didn't have to ask him to help me with God. He told me I should get my life straight with God before I do any of this stuff because without God my life would never get the focus it needs. He asked me to go home and pray about all this and resolve to get my life with God straight. 'First things first, Jimmie,' he said. Eddie, from what you told me, you know how to pray. I don't really know how to pray. Teach me, Eddie. Okay?"

So Eddie reminded Jimmie of the Our Father, the Hail Mary, and the Glory Be. "Mostly, Jimmie, talk to God as though you're talking to the best friend you have in the world. Because that's the truth, Jimmie, Jesus is the best friend we have. And start thinking of yourself as God's son. Talk to him as the Father that loves you, Jimmie, and that will be the right thing to do because that's who you are, and I am. Ask God to help you get a new life. Mostly, ask God to help you get to know him and to be part of your life each day from now on. And start going to mass again, Jimmie. That's where you can really begin to know about God and Jesus. One day I hope you will experience how much God loves you. In the meantime, believe that there is no greater love for you in life than the love God has for you."

Thus Jimmie's new life began, and he would be successful in being freed from drugs, just as Eddie was. Then he would join Eddie at school.

All of this happened just because Eddie told Jimmie what had happened to him and of the help he received from Fr. Ernesto and Sr. Peggy, and because Jimmie responded to the possibility that the same could happen to him. It did, except it was another sister who helped him—Sr. Teresa. Jimmie would never forget the help he received from Fr. Ernesto and Sr. Teresa. Jimmie, too, would come to know what it meant to love others and to be loved by others. He, too, developed his faith built on the love of God for him and for all. Jimmie's life was built step by step on the sure foundation of God and his love.

Stories help to bring the love of God to life in our imaginations and convey the experience of real life with God. But the stories don't live in isolation from God's own revelation about himself. It is this revelation that reveals the truth about God and what God intended in creating human beings.

Two principle statements of Jesus reveal God's intent. The first is this: You must love the Lord your God with all your heart, with all your soul, with all your mind, and with all your strength. The second is this: You must love your neighbor as yourself. And then Jesus adds: There is no commandment greater than these. [31]

All your heart, soul, mind, and strength. Nothing should be left out or held back. No half-measures or half-heartedness. God wants all of us, not just a part. And why not? He is the model of love, for he gave all for us to show us what love—authentic love—looks like.

But we know how weak we are; God does too. Nonetheless, in the face of all evidence to the contrary that we are capable of this, he asks us to love with everything within us. The great failure of Peter in his real love for Jesus shows us how much God understands our weakness. In the face of this, face-to-face with Peter, he tells Peter and us what the most important thing is.

> After the meal Jesus said to Simon Peter, "Simon, son of John, do you love me more than these others do?" He answered, "Yes Lord, you know I love you." Jesus said to him, "Feed my lambs." A second time he said to him, "Simon son of John, do you love me?" He replied, "Yes, Lord, you know I love you." Jesus said to him, "Look after my sheep." Then he said to him a third

31 Mark 12:30–31.

> time, "Simon son of John, do you love me?" Peter was upset that he asked him the third time, "Do you love me?" and said, "Lord, you know everything; you know I love you." Jesus said to him, "Feed my sheep."[32]

Even after Peter betrayed him, Jesus showed his love and forgiveness of Peter. And he told Peter what was even greater than his betrayal—his love for Christ. And Jesus connected this love to what he wanted of Peter—for him to feed his sheep. Jesus had already made Peter the primary leader ("You are Peter and on this rock I will build my Church"),[33] and now he was giving him the great commission: "Feed my sheep."

"Do you love me?" This is the great question for each of us. St. Paul repeated what the greatest is of faith, hope, and love.[34] Jesus narrowed it down and connected it to the first great commandment: to love God. He said it again:

> You must not set your hearts on things to eat and things to drink; nor must you worry. Your Father well knows you need them. No, set your hearts on the kingdom, and these other things will be given you as well. There is no need to be afraid, little flock, for it has pleased your Father to give you the kingdom.[35]

---

32 John 21:15–17.

33 Matthew 16:18.

34 1 Corinthians 13:13.

35 Luke 12:29–32.

Then, in describing this kingdom, Jesus said, "The kingdom of heaven is like treasure hidden in a field which someone has found. He goes off happy, sells everything he owns and buys the field."[36] The kingdom of God has this quality to it; there is nothing like it elsewhere. It is the fullness of life as best we can understand it. It is happiness to the full, which means that everything that contributes to happiness is present. Everything that makes life worth living is present. Everything that produces joy is there.

St. Paul tries to say it in these words:

> I believe nothing can happen that will outweigh the supreme advantage of knowing Christ Jesus my Lord. For him I have accepted the loss of everything, and I look on everything as so much rubbish if only I can have Christ, and be given a place in him.[37]
>
> We teach what scripture calls: the things that no eye has seen and no ear has heard, things beyond the mind of man, all that God has prepared for those who love him.[38]

We see love through our experience of it here on earth, but we see only partially. Even our partial seeing is clouded by the effects of sin in our lives, which have the effect of diminishing love. "Now we are seeing a dim reflection in a mirror; but then we shall be seeing face to face. The

36 Matthew 13:44.

37 Philippians 3:8–9.

38 1 Corinthians 2:9.

knowledge that I have now is imperfect; but then I shall know as fully as I am known."[39]

* * * * *

The things spoken of here are not just difficult for man; *they are impossible for man.* This may sound like bad news, but it is *the* good news. What is spoken of is made possible only with, in, and through Christ. Christ is "the Way, the Truth, and the Life."[40]

Are we any more astonished at hearing this than Jesus' disciples were? Jesus looked at the rich man who asked him what he must do to inherit eternal life. Jesus told him to follow the commandments but then looked deeper into the man and saw that he was attached to his wealth. "There is one thing you lack. Go and sell everything and give the money to the poor, and you will have treasure in heaven; then come follow me."[41] The man turned away because he had great wealth.

Isn't this us? The man had great wealth he was attached to for his security, his purpose, and likely his power. But we are all attached to the things of life, even if the things may not be material but intellectual. Fear of entering the unknown is a huge factor in entering a life where we give everything to God as he asks of us. The disciples were incredulous when they heard what Jesus said to the rich man.

---

39 1 Corinthians 13:12

40 John 14:6

41 Mark 10:17-22

> Jesus looked around and said to his disciples, "How hard it is for those who have riches to enter the kingdom of God!" The disciples were astounded by these words, but Jesus insisted, "My children," he said to them, "how hard it is to enter the kingdom of God! It is easier for a camel to pass through the eye of a needle[42] than for a rich man to enter the kingdom of God." They were more astonished than ever. "In that case," they said to one another, "who can be saved?" Jesus gazed at them. "For men," he said, "it is impossible, but not for God, because everything is possible for God."[43]

The truth is that only Christ makes entry into the kingdom of God possible.

> I am the vine, you are the branches. Whoever remains in me, with me in him, bears fruit in plenty; for cut off from me you can do nothing. As the Father has loved me so I have loved you. Remain in my love. If you keep my commandments you will remain in my love, just as I have kept my Father's commandments and remain in his love. I have told you this so that my own joy may be in you and your joy may be complete. This is my commandment: love one another, as I have loved you. [44]

---

42 A term denoting a small entrance designed to let people in and keep camels out.

43 Mark 10:23–27.

44 John 15:5.

What more can be said to establish the point? God created us so that we might share in his life. The life of God is filled with his love because God is love. God saw how we went about destroying our life with him after we decided, in the beginning, to separate ourselves from him. God created a people who would be his people and he their God. We see the nature of man at work in his inability to be faithful to God. "Come back to me, with all your heart," was the basic message of the prophets.

What does spiritual separation from God look like, and what does it take for God to save us from this condition? Listen to Ezekiel's description:

> The hand of Yahweh was laid on me, and he carried me away by the spirit of Yahweh and set me down in a valley, a valley full of bones. He said to me, "Son of man, can these bones live? Prophesy over these bones. Say, 'Dry bones, hear the word of Yahweh. The Lord Yahweh says to these bones: I am going to make my spirit enter you, and you will live.'"[45]

Ezekiel gives us these words, addressed to the house of Israel and to us.

> Then I am going to take you from among the nations and gather you together from the foreign countries, and bring you home to your own land. I shall pour clean water over you and you will be cleansed. I shall cleanse you of all your defilement and all

45 Ezekiel 1–5.

> your idols. I shall give you a new heart, and put a new spirit in you; I shall remove the heart of stone from your bodies and give you a heart of flesh instead. I shall put my spirit in you, and make you keep my laws and sincerely respect my observances.[46]

Here what God had in mind for us is clearly stated. Jesus tells us that he is the way by which this is to be accomplished, through life with, in, and through him. Without him we can do nothing.

God himself comes to us to make the life possible he alone can give. It is the life God intended for us from the beginning—eternal life. "And eternal life is this: to know you, the one true God, and Jesus Christ whom you have sent."[47]

What more could God have done for us out of his love for us? His love for us has provided the most intimate, love-filled life possible. We are God's beloved children, meant to know, love, and serve him in this life and be forever happy with him in the next.

46 Ezekiel 36:24–27.

47 John 17:3.

Epilogue

Ah, but what about Ed and Shelley? What became of them?

Ed and Shelley continued to read and reflect on *Why Love?* As they did, they found themselves being drawn more and more toward God. It wasn't just that they understood more but that what they read was connecting to their life experiences. The things said about love—especially the love within family—spoke directly to their experience. Indeed, it almost sounded like common sense to them. They were able to begin connecting to the love of God through their sharing together and through their prayer. Because of the connection to their life experience, what was written simply struck them as the truth.

It was this quality that most attracted them. Ed's original question to Fr. Jim was, "How can I get the right answers? How will I know I'm not spinning my wheels, wasting my time?" Fr. Jim had answered, "Let me begin with a question: how would one determine truth?" It was the truth Ed was seeking, and later so was Shelley. It was this aspect of the book that rang out to them. It sounded true, it felt true, and it was true to their life experience. The further they went into the book, the more they came to believe it was true. Each of them felt they had come to something they wanted to become part of and wanted to make part of their own lives and their children's lives. They believed the central proclamation of the book: God is love. They wanted their family to live life *within* that love.

As they proceeded through the book, they decided to get their children involved with some of the questions so they too could begin to join them in their journey. This served to introduce the children to what their parents were doing and to the change in their lives that was in process.

After they had finished the book, they went back to see Fr. Ben and, after some discussion, told him they wanted to enter the RCIA in order to become Catholics. They told Fr. Ben they wanted the fullness of life spoken of in the book that was made possible when Christ created his church. They wanted to receive the Lord in the Eucharist, to expose themselves on a continuous basis to his Word, and to be able to receive Christ's forgiveness through his sacrament of reconciliation. They had come to understand the role of the priesthood and the nature of authority within the church through apostolic succession. Even before they entered the RCIA, they had an understanding of these things.

When they entered the RCIA, they never expected to find such richness within the community of the church. The facilitators opened up the Scripture to them in such a gentle and satisfying way. They came to understand what baptism would mean to them and their children, and to their whole future. When they had completed the RCIA and entered into full communion with the church at the Easter vigil, they were filled with the joy that comes with understanding what they had done and what had been done to them. They were immersed in Christ, and they had begun the fullness of their life with him, exactly as he provided for in the beginning of the church two thousand years ago and has been providing ever since. On that same night, their children entered the church as well. They were now a family in Christ.

But we need to skip forward thirty years to see what became of Ed and Shelley and their family. By this time, each of the children had married and begun families of their own. Each of the children married within the church and were bringing their children up to be Catholic. Had what was proclaimed in *Why Love?* come true for them? Had they discovered that it was true and that it stood the test of time? Had they discovered it had stood the test of the questions of their family and friends? Had they discovered its truth even through the most difficult periods in their lives?

To all of these questions, the answer was an unequivocal yes. To show this to be true, let's look at their life thirty years later.

The first evidence of the penetration of their lives by the love of God was in the different bond that formed between Ed and Shelley. The bond they had before Ed began his search for answers was one of commitment to one another and trust in one another. Their relationship was based on the belief that the other would be there through thick and thin and their mutual commitment would see them through whatever life would present to them.

But what they didn't have—and what they never imagined becoming a part of their lives together—was faith in God, hope in God, and actually coming to know the God who loves them. This difference developed over the thirty years that passed. They came to know God in very personal ways—each in his or her own different way, but each in a way that made each know who he or she was. They came to know what it meant to be children of the Father, brother and sister of Christ, part of the body of Christ, and souls wherein dwelt the Holy Spirit.

It would be this constant knowledge of the presence of God in their lives—the constant presence of the Father, the Son, and the Holy Spirit—that would form the backbone of their lives individually and together. This would be true of their children as well, as they soon developed into a family in Christ. All of them had learned how to pray, how to pray together, and how to turn to God for every need. All of this created the most intense bond in Christ between them. This was a life Ed and Shelley could never have imagined before entering it.

They became part of their parish community, and both of them became part of the RCIA team, passing on to others what had been so richly passed on to them. They got to know personally many of those in the parish, and they formed a particularly deep friendship with one couple they got to know because their children had common interests. It was with this couple that they first discovered the incredible value of sharing their faith. They never knew what a rich, ongoing source of grace this would be. The result was that the two families formed a very special bond built on the love of God for each of them. Because of their sharing together, they became even more aware of God's presence in their lives each day, and it was a constant source of inspiration and joy to them.

Having this daily life with God didn't save them from difficulty in life. They were subject to the same ups and downs in life common to most. They experienced the deaths of their parents; two close friends died tragically during that time; Ed suffered the loss of his job, and they consequently lost their home; one of the children became involved with a bad crowd for a time and was a great worry to them; and Shelley had to have a significant operation that had everyone concerned.

But these were not things that overwhelmed them or altered their daily life with Christ, his church, and God their Father. They knew the power of the Holy Spirit at work in them; they knew God's abiding, loving presence in their lives, and they placed all their trust in him. If anything, these events only strengthened their faith, their family, and their love for God and each other because of the clear evidence of his presence among them. By this time, their faith was rock-like. Nothing in their lives could separate them from the love of God made visible in Christ.[48]

The greatest change came in their hearts. Before they came into this life in Christ, they were more or less oblivious to many things in life. They weren't that aware of their friends and neighbors as to whom they really were in life. They weren't aware of the needs of others or of the good they could do for others. Their perspective in life was narrow, confined mostly to family and work. Nor were

---

48 Romans 8:38–39: "For I am certain of this: neither death nor life, no angel, no prince, nothing that exists, nothing still to come, not any power, or height or depth, nor any created thing, can ever come between us and the love of God made visible in Christ Jesus our Lord."

they aware of each other's spiritual needs or those of their children.

But now they tried as best they could to follow God's call in their lives. This extended from how they raised their children to what work they would spend their lives at. For example, as a consequence of the loss of Ed's job, he took the time to pray about his future and to do so in communion with Shelley. The result was that Ed redirected his work life to where he believed God was calling him. Shelley was able to affirm that where she worked was where God wanted her. Each of them had the peace of heart that comes from knowing they were blooming where God had planted them and the knowledge that, that being so, he would provide for all their needs.

But beyond the essentials in life, they directed their free time to helping others who were like they had been—people who didn't have faith but were now searching for faith just as they had. Also, because of that near-death of their oldest child, they began to help out at that hospital in the area of child illness and death, doing what they could to support families in distress. This was because their hearts had taken on love for others as children of God. They tried to see Christ in each person in their lives and to treat them accordingly. They had developed "hearts of flesh."

The greatest thing that changed in their lives, and in the lives of their children, was that they placed God first. They had come to know with certainty that when God is placed first and when all trust is placed in him, everything flows from that. He was their Father and they his children, and they lived in that conviction and spirit. This was a conviction of the heart that had been firmly planted in them by the action of the Holy Spirit within them. It was more than an act of the will. It was the consequence of the love of God they had experienced and come to understand deeply. Before, during, and after any issue in their lives was God and his love. It was within this environment of the love of God that they lived and moved and had their being. This permeation of their lives by the love of God transformed their hearts, minds, and spirits. They had, in effect, become "other Christs" in the body of Christ.

"I have come so that they may have life and have it to the full."[49] This was the life Jesus had spoken of, and Ed and Shelley had come to know this fullness in their lives. It was life filled with love and meaning and purpose. It was life filled with the hope of eternal life with God.

When they grew old and experienced the difficulties of old age, they remained filled with the same spirit, the same fullness. They had learned how to use these trials to further God's purposes; they had learned how to unite any infirmity with the suffering of Christ and thereby turn these things into advantages. In this way, the love of Christ permeated all their comings and goings.

It would be Shelley who would die first. As she became ill, she and Ed knew the hope of the last stage of life. They knew the love of God they had been part of for all these years, and they knew that this was just a glimmer of the love they would know in heaven. Thus her final days were filled with this hope and expectation.

On the night before she died, she and Ed had a few moments together. "Ed," she said, "thank you for the life you brought us into. If you hadn't tried to find the meaning

---

49 John 10:10.

of our daughter's life, we may never have come into life with God. Look what it has meant to us. We could never have imagined a life like we have had. We wouldn't have believed anyone if they had tried to tell us life could be like this. Ed, we have loved each other as much as we can even imagine. How wonderful it has been."

After Shelley died, Ed lived in the peace and joy of knowing where Shelley was, and he, his children, and his grandchildren looked forward to the day when they would meet again in the full presence of God. She had told them all she would be their saint in heaven, praying for them. All of them lived in this belief and included her in their daily prayers, asking her to pray for so-and-so or for such-and-such situation. Nothing of importance was excluded from their daily prayers, and they were certain nothing of importance was excluded from hers.

The same spirit of love and hope prevailed when Ed died. The children and grandchildren held him in their hearts with love for the rest of their days. Can life be more permeated with love than this?

From the beginning of their life with God, their lives were full of love. Ed and Shelley knew the love of God for them and lived in that love.

Glory be to the Father, to the Son, and to the Holy Spirit, as it was in the beginning, is now, and ever shall be.

Amen.

CPSIA information can be obtained at www.ICGtesting.com
Printed in the USA
LVOW050727270213

321809LV00001B/12/P